Praise for

"The *Vikings of the New World Saga* contains some of the most profound characterization I have ever read. Inlaid with both tension and turmoil, romance and redemption, like its predecessor *God's Daughter*, *Forest Child* takes the reader on a journey that is anything but gentle—yet unrivaled in its poignancy. With each turn of the page, hearts are searched and the love of a mighty God has the power to triumph. By illuminating the lives of a pagan culture, we readers are given a profound reminder that our souls are of the same make as the Vikings'. The weapons we wield may not be of iron or steel, but they are just as powerful, and though our choices may not affect a village of loved ones, to seek goodness and wisdom is a call that stretches across even centuries of time. Set within a most stunning landscape, and filled with a genuine cast of characters, *Forest Child* is a heart-wrenching portrayal of love and humanity and one that will hold a special place in my heart."
~ **Joanne Bischof**, award-winning author of *The Lady and the Lionheart*

"It's the rare book that draws me in so fully that I respond with gasps and tears and a quickened heart rate. It's the best kind of book that makes me forget about the dishes in the sink and the meals that need to be made. It's my favorite kind of book which keeps me up late into the night with a strong desire to find out what happens next.

Forest Child by Heather Day Gilbert is such a book.

It's no exaggeration to say that I've waited two years for this book. My patience paid off. Freydis is well rounded, complex, her character so very real in her fierceness and vulnerability. The plot moves, keeping the reader turning page after page, unable to abandon the story. From the first page to the last, the reader is engaged with the characters.

Whatever you do, don't miss this book."
~**Susie Finkbeiner**, author of *A Cup of Dust: A Novel of the Dust Bowl*

"*Forest Child* is one of the bravest works of fiction I've ever read. Brimming with tension, yet laced with tenderness, this powerful saga is sure to keep you turning the pages far into the night. An ingenious blend of Viking history and timeless issues of the heart still relevant today."
-**Jocelyn Green**, award-winning author of the *Heroines Behind the Lines* series

"In *Forest Child*, Heather Day Gilbert has written a strong heroine that epitomizes the term against an intimate and unflinching tale revealing remarkable historical detail, dark family secrets, and a cast of characters that left an indelible influence on the spread of the Christian faith."
-**Nancy Kimball**, author of *Chasing the Lion*

"Using the same vivid first-person, present-tense that she used in *God's Daughter*, Heather brought me straight into the Viking world of Freydis, a tough-shelled woman with a bleeding heart. The profoundly redemptive message of this story - the real-life themes - the characters portrayed so well that they keep coming to my mind days later… This is a starkly beautiful, realistic historical novel about the authentic transformation that Jesus Christ can bring to those who call on the Name of the Lord. I highly recommend that you put this one on your to-read list for the fall!"
-**Alicia G. Ruggieri**, author of *All Our Empty Places*

"In *Forest Child*, Heather Day Gilbert takes the reader deep enough into the thoughts of Freydis that her emotions and her actions become equally riveting as the story progresses. The extraordinary tales from a vastly different, often dark culture become personal, relatable, and ultimately hopeful."
-**Christina Coryell**, *USA Today* bestselling author

"*Forest Child*. An enthralling Viking tale coupled with the heart-rending journey of a troubled soul.

Fierce, inscrutable Freydis Eiriksdottir grabbed my heart and didn't let go. I loved her even as I deplored her actions, mourned for her brokenness, and ultimately rejoiced in her transformation. Heather Gilbert has once again brought the Vikings to larger-than-life in the pages of *Forest Child* with authentic historical detail, a captivating story, and an unforgettable heroine."

~**Stephanie Landsem**, author of *The Living Water Series*

"Fierce in protecting her family, vulnerable in her refusal to accept love, Freydis the forest child is a heroine like no other. In the end, the weight of her own story—its brutality and loneliness—crushes her. But in that crushing, redemption whispers.

This is what historical fiction should be—a breathtaking journey to a distant time and place with characters whose stories touch our hearts and whose joys and sorrows are, at their core, very much like our own."

~**Karin Kaufman**, author of the *Anna Denning* series

"*Forest Child* is a well written story of survival and hope, betrayal and forgiveness. Deep characters as rich and savage as Viking history, this novel is a testament that love, courage, and faith are timeless. A must read for historical fiction fans."

~**Peter Leavell**, award-winning novelist & historian

FOREST CHILD

Vikings of the New World Saga
Book Two

HEATHER DAY GILBERT

Heather Day Gilbert

Forest Child
By Heather Day Gilbert

Copyright 2016 Heather Day Gilbert

ISBN: 978-0-9978279-0-3

Cover Design by Jenny at Seedlings Design Studio
Illustrations by Jon Day
Interior Formatting by Polgarus Studio

Published by WoodHaven Press

All rights reserved. No part of this publication may be reproduced in any form, stored in any retrieval system, posted on any website, or transmitted in any form or by any means, without written permission from the publisher, except for brief quotations in printed reviews and articles.

Series: Gilbert, Heather Day. Vikings of the New World Saga; 2
Subject: Vikings—North America—Fiction
North America—Discovery and Exploration—Fiction
Genre: Historical Fiction

Author Information: heatherdaygilbert.com

Other Books by Heather Day Gilbert:

God's Daughter, Book One in the
Vikings of the New World Saga

Miranda Warning, Book One in
A Murder in the Mountains Series

Trial by Twelve, Book Two in
A Murder in the Mountains Series

Out of Circulation, Book One in the
Hemlock Creek Suspense Series

*Indie Publishing Handbook:
Four Key Elements for the Self-Publisher*

Author's Note: To be Read

I have wrestled with this novel for two years now, unsure how to faithfully bring Freydis' story to the page. I did not know what would have driven a grown woman to take the extreme actions Freydis, according to the sagas, took. There are parts of this story I did not want to write, did not want to even visualize, and yet I had to, to stay true to the Viking sagas, because Freydis was a real person. So was her husband, and her family. This is truly historical, biographical fiction.

When I finally began to write in earnest, as so often happens, the words began to come. The blanks began to be filled. Is everything in this story true? No. Just like *God's Daughter,* this novel aligns with the sagas as best it can, but I had to fill in the character backgrounds and motivations fictionally. In other words, the bones are solid, but I have fleshed out the rest, based on hints the sagas have given me...like the fact that Gudrid was drop-dead gorgeous and quite a catch (she had three husbands) or that Leif could be harsh, or that Freydis was...well, Freydis.

When I wrote *God's Daughter,* I spent hours checking and cross-checking the actual words I utilized, trying to stick mostly with nouns, verbs, adjectives, and adverbs that had an Old Norse equivalent. Let it be known that with this story, although I am indeed cross-checking terminology, I have decided to err on the side of readability and flow, rather than rigorous faithfulness to the Old Norse. Here's why: I believe Vikings would have *said* something equivalent to "vomit," for instance, but that word *itself* might not have come into play until years later. However, you are probably reading this novel in English, and therefore, although I do try to primarily use Old Norse word equivalents, I am leaning more on words that you, as a reader, would recognize today, therefore giving myself a bit more play with the vocabulary. Yes, I have tried not to sound anachronistic, at least with objects that wouldn't have existed in the Norse world around AD 1000. I am trying not to throw you, the reader, out of the story altogether. But as you know, I prefer writing my historicals in first person, present tense, which is rare in historical novels. So we're already walking on the edge here. Why not just dive right in?

Also, when it comes to historicity, although I do my research, when something the sagas say contradicts the historical information available to me right now, I will *most often* err on the side of the sagas. Why? Because that is what this series *is*: a retelling of the *Sagas of the Greenlanders*. That is my guidebook, basically. Also because, time after time, I have seen things historians have initially poo-pooed about the sagas finally coming to light as being historically sound. Things like red-haired Skraelings in North America, for instance, or trees growing in Greenland around the time of the sagas.

Finally, there are violent scenes in this book. There is a scene that actually turned my stomach each time I read it. It is not a pleasant scene, but it is a necessary one. Freydis does not have a gentle story, because she was not a gentle woman. And as we know, times were different then, and just... *Vikings*. Although I have worked hard with the *Vikings of the New World Saga* to show the family-oriented, loving side of the Vikings, I would be completely disingenuous if I never showed the grittier, violent side. And, as much as I wanted to protect her from it as I wrote, Freydis had a violent story. I had to let her live it for us.

This book takes a long, hard look at themes like vengeance and murder. I have always liked *The Count of Monte Cristo*, yet even as we mentally cheer him on in his vengeful machinations to those who deserve it, at the same time, we lament with him at the lingering regret he inflicts on himself in the process. And though we might not like it, the truth is that there *can be* redemption for murderers, just like for any other sinners.

If you really want to understand what I have done with *God's Daughter* and *Forest Child*, I beg of you, read *The Sagas of the Greenlanders* (especially before reviewing this book harshly). Those who have read the sagas understand what I have done with these stories. Yes, there are some tweaks in my books so I can get the timelines or maps to match up. Yes, many of the *Thor*_____ names have been changed so the readers can better follow the storyline (Ref's name, for instance). But the bottom line is that I wanted to bring the sagas to life for my generation—because I'm allegedly related to the characters in these stories (Thorvald Eiriksson), and you might be, as well.

I do hope you enjoy reading of this real Viking woman who sailed to North America and did things that would go down in history, both for good and for evil. And Freydis—you have walked with me for so long. I hope I got even half your story right.

-Heather

Please note that if you prefer a visual of how the characters are connected to Freydis and to each other, there is a family tree at the end of this book. There is also a glossary of foreign terms for easy reference.

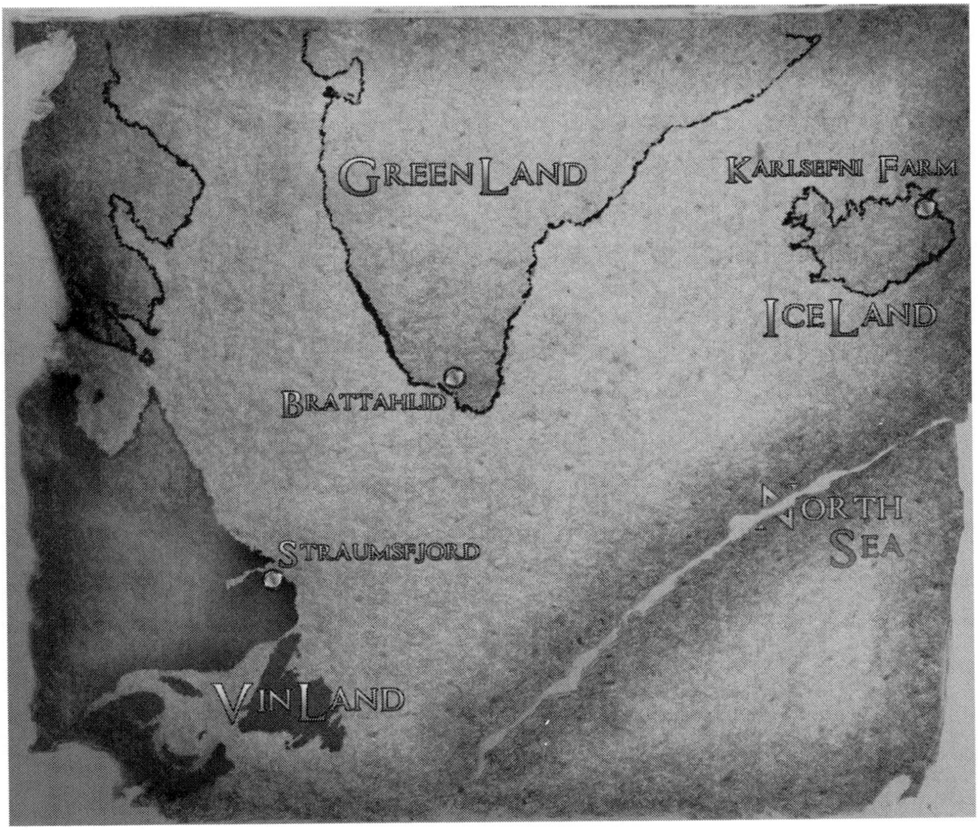
GreenLand
Karlsefni Farm
IceLand
Brattahlid
North
Sea
Straumsfjord
VinLand

Dedicated to my fellow warrior-spirit author, Becky, who wields her pen as precisely as Freydis wields her knife.

And to my readers, who prayed me through the tough scenes in this story and wouldn't let me shirk from writing it. You are such an encouragement to me.

"We brothers will never be a match for your ill-will."
(Helgi, the Icelandic sailor, to Freydis)
-The Saga of the Greenlanders

"She (Freydis) was a domineering woman…She had been married to him mainly for his money."
-The Saga of the Greenlanders

Prologue
Eiriksfjord, Greenland

THE WHISPERS FILLED ALL her silences.

Forest child. That's Eirik's forest child.

Freydis followed her brothers' tracks in the light snow, determined to find them. They never let her win at games. Even though they'd only seen a few winters more than her six, they acted like they were the only ones who knew how to fight.

Everything was a competition for them. But they wouldn't compete with her, even though Father had made her a sword and a shield when she was only four.

Today she would prove them wrong.

She sniffed the air, then sighed at the cleanness of it. No more fishy seaweed smell drifting up from the shore. No more summer jumps into the waterfall pond. Sunlight would be filtered through the hole in the roof, and she'd have to sit indoors with her stepmother and spin.

She could almost feel her stepmother's scolding eyes, the same blue as the layer beneath the ice. Ice inside and out, all year long. She was not her real mother, even though she had adopted her from her unmarried mother.

A twig cracked nearby. Freydis' red hair spilled out of the leather band she'd hastily wrapped around it. She shoved the curls out of her eyes, wooden sword at the ready.

Arms wrapped around her. Those cheaters. She jabbed her elbow back, but he'd already grabbed her sword.

Thorstein thrust his equally red head over her shoulder. "You weren't watching, foolish girl!"

Leif ran out of the woods, light yellow hair flying. Freydis dropped her eyes. She didn't mind Thorstein's taunts, but Leif's size scared her sometimes. He was built like a tree, and he knew it.

If only Thorvald were home. He looked out for her. But he had to sail with Father this time.

Thorstein shoved her forward, pinning her arms behind her. "What is the penalty, m'lord?"

Leif laughed. "Let's put this forest child where she belongs—in the forest."

They marched Freydis straight ahead, into the trees. Chill seeped into her hands, but she wouldn't cry out.

"I have some rope." Thorstein nodded to the loop on his belt.

Leif looked thoughtful. "She's quite crafty—she could get out."

"Let's put her up a tree! She'll never get down!" Thorstein talked as if Freydis couldn't hear.

She stopped and stomped on his foot, hard. This game wasn't fun at all.

"You! You…forest child!" As Thorstein hopped around, Freydis broke free and ran toward the longhouse. Leif blocked her path.

"Not so fast, you red-headed demon. We're going to take the fire out of you!"

As each brother grabbed an arm, they dragged her back into the woods. Leif made fast work of climbing the tree, Thorstein's length of rope between his teeth. Thorstein pulled a short knife from his belt sheath and pointed it at her back. "Get up, you wild girl!"

The game was over. She was deliberately slow as she climbed the tree, finally nestling into the wider spot where Leif stood. She wanted to bite him as he tied her to the trunk, but what if she lost her balance and fell onto Thorstein's knife?

Leif slid back down and landed with a thud. As her brothers walked away, clapping each other's backs, Freydis wondered. Should she be afraid, sitting in a tree, in the quick-darkening woods? Should she care that she'd had no mid-day meal and that her hands were tingling?

She decided not.

The next morning, the slaves found her, asleep in the tree. Hawk's feathers were scattered on the snow beneath her. She'd remembered the knife in her boot and had cut her ties, killed the bird, and eaten its raw flesh. For warmth, she had wrapped its carcass around her hands.

She refused to leave the tree until her father, Eirik the Red, and her brother Thorvald returned. That was three days later.

She'd turned her brothers' disdain to her favor—now they knew she was the most determined of Eirik's children.

And they could ignore her no longer.

PART ONE

Vinland (Upper North America)

Circa AD 1000

ONE

WHEN ANGER OVERTAKES ME, I struggle against my first instinct—the instinct to kill everything in sight.

Right now, as I stare down a pagan holy woman, I feel that relentless urge. Blood rushes to my fingertips, silently pushing me to take up a weapon. I sense where my curved knife hangs in its leather loop on my belt. In one heartbeat, I could slit her throat like the coward she is.

Valdis saves her jeers for when her husband is away. Today the men are collecting wood for winter, so only the women have gathered in the longhouse for our mid-day meal. Finnbogi has never seen his wife's hostile behavior, but he would doubtless excuse it and bow to her wishes as he always does.

She positions herself at meals so her young woman followers—like fox kits on a teat—can sit and lap up her words of wisdom. Even now, she has taken the most ornately carved chair at the head of the long table, where she glares at me with her frozen seaweed eyes.

"Eirik's daughter Freydis is like her father. She must have her own way." Her light, lilting voice barely masks the repulsion underneath. She smoothes her curtain of ice-blonde hair. Her fingers drop to her ever-present staff, which now leans against her chair. The curved rod has an amber ball atop it. As if amber were any rare jewel. I would be more impressed if it were a seeing stone. Then I would steal it for our voyage back.

I force my gaze elsewhere. Gudrid would tell me it is beneath me to reply to a woman like this, a woman so determined to inflame my anger. My own husband Ref would say that she is no one to worry about.

But I know better.

My sister-in-law Gudrid is not here with me in Vinland. And Ref has no say in my behavior. He never has.

I slide my chair back and stand. Like a large cat, I prowl behind the others until I stand directly behind Valdis' chair. One of the young women with unusually black hair opens her mouth, as if pushing out a mute scream.

I lean down and yank the hair away from Valdis' soft white ear. It is so pale, it looks bloodless. And yet if I cut it, it would still bleed.

I drop my voice to a purr. "It is so kind of you to show interest in my family. Perhaps since you are so familiar with my father's ways, you also remember what Eirik the Red did to those who double-crossed him."

Valdis does not flinch. I must admit she has an imposing presence. She grips her staff as if it could aid her.

I speak loudly into her ear, forcing her to squirm away. "Pray all you like, *volva*. The gods are deaf in this land. You will see that soon enough."

Grabbing my rough skirts, I whirl out the longhouse door. Why do we allow this ungrateful Icelandic crew to share our buildings? Leif set up this beautiful camp when he sailed to Vinland a few years ago, so by rights it should be mine while we are here. But the Icelanders managed to outstrip my ship and unload before our crew made shore.

Outside, I run directly into my husband. Ref catches my arms with his sturdy hands and I glare down at him. He stands a bit shorter than I do, so I straighten to my full height.

"It has not even been a month, and still the Icelandic women taunt me," I complain.

As is his way, my husband takes his time responding. I study his striking, mismatched eyes—one green, one blue—as if they hide the perfect solution. And yet I know he will offer no advice. Impatience overtakes me and I shove him away.

"Did you hear me? Those Icelanders will mutiny on us yet!"

His voice finds purchase and he takes a step closer. "You are prepared for that."

He speaks of the extra men I brought with us, thus breaking my pact with the Icelandic sailors. We had agreed to thirty fighting men each, but I hid five warriors in weapons chests on our ship—warriors who were especially loyal to me because I held their freedom in my hands.

I cross my arms. "Yes. It is I who was prepared, and not you. It is I who saw an opportunity and grasped it, as I always do. It is never you. You simply trail after me like a wave in the wake of a ship."

Ref's gaze drifts to the sky. This is how he reacts to all my impassioned statements. My father was not this way. He would have showed concern. He would have brought pain to those who hurt me.

With the exception of my brothers. They could do no wrong.

Finnbogi and his brother, Helgi, stride toward the longhouse. Men begin to pour out of the forest, weary from their labors.

"Freydis." Finnbogi dips his head to me, long white hair spilling over his shoulders.

All these Icelanders look alike, the brothers in particular. I cannot tell them apart, save when their sleeves are pushed back. Helgi has a scar running the length of his arm, which speaks to his more aggressive nature.

Helgi does not acknowledge me now. I overcome my urge to kick some respect into him.

Instead, I plant a kiss on Ref's lips. The men laugh at his surprised look, but I want to make it clear that we are a unit. Ref is always on my side.

I pat Ref's shoulder. "I will meet you in our house." My tone is charged with desire I don't feel.

Ref grabs for my hand, holding it fast. His eyes search my face, unsure. I force a smile and he is convinced. "I will be there soon," he says.

My men follow behind the Icelanders, wood chips flecking their tunics and trousers. Why do they not lead this party instead of falling behind like they are shamed?

As Ref walks inside, my youngest stowaway, Atli, meets my gaze. His eyes are a clear blue, like my own. My half-brother, Leif, brought the fatherless boy back from Norway, and Atli has grown into one of the fiercest fighters I have ever seen. A smile curves my lips as I imagine the grand and mighty Leif Eiriksson, crying over the loss of his favorite warrior.

Filled with goodwill, I clap Atli on the back. "How were your ventures today? Perhaps you are becoming dulled by your tedious wood chopping? Come hunting with me later."

Atli looks hesitantly after the chattering men in the longhouse. "Finnbogi thought I should stack wood."

I spit on the ground near his boots. "Finnbogi has no say in what my men do. Let him stack his own wood. You need to hone your hunting skills so we can prepare for winter."

Smiling, he nods. As he steps over the threshold, one of Valdis' women deliberately bumps into him with her hip. She suggestively runs a hand through his long blond hair.

I catch Valdis' hooded look as she observes the encounter. That volva is plotting something, I can feel it. When her eyes flick to me, brimming with challenge, my jaw tightens. I have made a decision.

Stamping back into the longhouse, I freeze like a hawk in the door frame until everyone looks at me. Ref's spoon stops in mid-air, soup dribbling onto his trim gray-and-white beard.

"Finnbogi and Helgi." My taut voice stabs into the silence. "Although you arrived first, you were well aware that this camp belongs to my brother, Leif. Why did you unload your belongings here?"

Finnbogi's pale, barely-visible eyebrows shoot up. "We thought you were going to keep your word to us. We agreed to provide the ships and you would share the housing in Vinland."

Valdis places her tiny hand on her husband's arm and gives me a look that could freeze water. These Icelanders lust for more than plunder—they want power. I know it.

But I have the power here. And I have the final say.

"Leif lent me these houses. Not you."

Helgi throws his bowl against the wall right next to me, spattering the packed dirt floor with watery soup and pottery shards.

He rasps, "We brothers will never be a match for your ill-will." Motioning for his crew, he charges toward me.

Of course, Ref sits frozen to his bench. But Atli jumps to my side and draws his sword. Another of my stowaways, tall and immobile as a frost-giant, protectively flanks me.

My curved knife is snug in hand when Helgi draws near, its metal loop on my smallest finger.

"If you attack me, you attack Leif Eiriksson," I say.

"Hiding behind your brother, Freydis?" Helgi huffs. "We both know he must despise you after stealing half his slaves for this voyage. Besides, the ships are ours."

Finnbogi comes to his brother's side. "Ours," he repeats.

Valdis sneers behind her husband's back as if victory is in hand. In a way, it is. If we have no ship, we cannot sail home. Ref is a skilled wood-worker, but to create an entire *knarr* during the winter would be nearly impossible.

Ref carefully sets his spoon down and stands. No one looks at him. My men's eyes are on me, waiting for a sign to attack.

Today we are not prepared. I prefer to fight in the open, not in the closeness of a longhouse. Outside, the trees can come to my aid, as they always do.

But I will not drop my knife first. I glare into Helgi's cruel eyes. "You may own the ships, but my brother owns the houses. You go and build your own."

Silence falls. Finnbogi finally claps a hand on his brother's shoulder. "Let us not fight her." The unspoken word *now* hovers in the air after his last word.

Helgi's lips flatten. "Very well. We will build our own longhouse, where your crew will not be welcome."

I sheathe my knife and lighten my tone. "Best wishes to you."

Valdis and her women sweep past me like a cold breeze. I clasp my hands so I don't accidentally grab her staff and trip her.

The men slowly return to their soup, but Ref moves to my side. Instead of asking questions or chiding me, he simply glowers like a cornered bear.

My husband is so unlike me. I will never be cornered. There is always a way to stop your enemy.

As the proverb says, *A cleaved head never plots.*

TWO

BACK IN OUR SMALL hut, I start pacing. Ref enters, throwing a few pine cones and twigs onto the fire to keep it going. There is no avoiding it: the days have turned cold.

I speak as I walk, trying to clear my head. "Ref, that woman is evil. You refuse to see it. And look at those women she brought. The last thing we need is beautiful young women to turn our men's heads from their tasks. You remember what happened at Straumsfjord."

"She's his wife." He holds a piece of wood up to the light, lovingly tracing its grain. He will probably carve it with serpents or twining grapevines.

"This means nothing. Most men travel without their wives."

"I don't." He tosses the stick into the fire.

"You couldn't." I laugh, but he keeps his back turned, silent.

I hook the hot water pot from the fire, then dip some out and mix it with cold water in a bucket in the corner. If there's one thing Gudrid beat into my head, it's the fact that ladies bathe. I'll use any means possible to intimidate the ice out of Valdis, to compete on her level. I pull off my overdress and shift and strip down, taking a rag from the chair. Just as I thought, Ref's eyes can't stay on the fire.

Most men are easy to control. But women, with their deep loyalties, know how to cover their intentions with smiles. They may be slow to aim the arrow, but when they let it fly, they'll hit the heart every time.

Lying on our makeshift bed, I finger my silver Midgard serpent armband. Ref gave it to me before we married, impressing me not only with his wealth, but with his insight into my love of sailing. The carved beast, biting its golden tail, represents the circular seas of the earth.

As my husband idly strokes my arm, I remind myself why I sailed for Vinland so soon after returning from our last expedition with Thorfinn Karlsefni.

I watched my brother accept Thorfinn's gifts of grapes, wheat, and wood, even though he's jealous of the man. Leif is easily bought.

Now that two of my brothers are dead, Leif and I are the last living children of Eirik the Red. I should have equal say in the family farm. Did my brothers know what Father told me—that I was like a son to him and that I deserved the same privileges as his sons?

I know what Leif would say if I claimed such a right. "You are nothing but a forest child, Freydis. Your mother was a mistress, not a wife."

Ref traces my chin. "You are thoughtful."

He should know by now that I am always thinking. Always planning.

He continues. "You are thinking of Brattahlid. I have seen that look before."

I roll over, unwilling to let him see my eyes fill with tears. I hate weakness.

He runs a strong hand up my arm, then grips it firmly, as if tethering me to the ground. "We have our own farm, Freydis. It is nearly the size of Brattahlid. So why is it never enough?"

"I should own my father's farm. He intended for me to have it. He knew I was the strongest of all his children. In very truth, he left me his helmet to show his preference, but of course that was not enough for Leif. And Thjodhild would never come to my side on this. She has always preferred her own sons."

Ref's eyes soften a bit. "With my wealth and the plunder from Vinland, you will be able to buy half of Brattahlid."

I don't want my husband's wealth. My own plunder should be enough to purchase half the farm…if I can store some goods on Finnbogi's ship. That way Leif will have to recognize my authority. Already, several of my brother's slaves are now loyal to me.

When Ref remains silent, I glance at him. The sides of his head are shaved. Gray-and-white hair forms a messy comb that falls over his forehead. He gives me the same unsure look he always does, one that says he is willing to do whatever I ask.

It is the look of a hunted animal.

I stand, pulling my linen shift down over my head. "I promised Atli I would train with him today."

Ref helps me as I put on my blue overdress. "The boy is learning quickly. I have been teaching him to carve, as well."

I push one of my silver brooches into the woolen overdress strap.

Ref speaks of Atli as if he were his son. I think of the son he did have—our baby who was born dead in Straumsfjord.

Perhaps my sadness shows, because Ref pulls me into a hug. I allow myself to remain still as long as I can before pulling away.

I don't need him. I don't need anyone.

My large stowaway, Thorgrim, greets me outside our hut. "Helgi and Finnbogi have taken our wood to build their longhouse."

The wood we were going to take back to Greenland as plunder.

He continues, anxiety charging his deep voice. "Also, two men have sailed here in a small boat. They speak our language, yet one looks like a Skraeling. They asked after you and Thorfinn Karlsefni."

He points toward our inlet, where a narrow longboat, so small it would only hold a few men, lies overturned on the sand. I have seen this kind of boat once before. It is what the native Skraelings used when they attacked our camp at Straumsfjord.

Silently, he leads me to the longhouse. I slip through the door, curved knife in hand. Two men, one with light and one with dark hair, sit at the table facing away from me. This is an unprotected position that shows an unwarranted trust.

I prowl up behind the larger blond man and press my knife to his throat. "What do you want?"

"Freydis Eiriksdottir," he says.

I thrust my face toward his, taking in his square jaw and pale eyes. I look at his companion and my breath stops.

These are the men who stayed behind at Straumsfjord. Tyr, Leif's blond warrior, and Suka, Leif's native Greenlandic slave. I never thought they would survive, much as I dreamed one of them would.

The one who claimed to love me.

Suka raises a thick eyebrow. "Freydis." His teeth are so white in his smooth tan skin. He smells familiar and solid, like fresh-cut wood. The days after my son's death were a blur, but I remember Suka stayed with me in the woods while I recovered. We slept on the same leaf bed in a cave. Did I make myself vulnerable to him? Did he take what he had so obviously wanted from me?

My memory is faulty. The *berserker* mushrooms I ate during those dark days tore holes in my memory. I stand still, embarrassed under his steady dark gaze.

Tyr stands, a head taller than I am. "I will speak with Ref."

We are alone. I drop to the bench beside Suka, drawn to him as I always am. I touch his long hair, which is obviously unwashed.

His warm gaze caresses my curls, then travels to my face, but he does not touch me. Yet he mutters something that sounds like *my fire*.

This can never be. And yet part of me longs to know what happened between us.

Because I am carrying a child, and I am afraid it might be his.

THREE

I SAW SUCH BEAUTIFUL things with the mushrooms. I heard voices that were not even human, like *valkyrie*. Gudrid took my mushroom supply and locked it in her box, although that did not stop me from breaking the lock and taking what I wanted.

Yet when the mushrooms' wonders began to give me after-effects I could not escape, I chose to leave them behind in Greenland. Although the mushrooms also grow here in Vinland, I pretend they do not.

Ref hardly knows why I react as I do now—sudden noises make me too alert, ready to attack, so I retreat into the woods for the natural quiet the trees provide. My anger strikes without warning, flaring like a volcanic plume.

And yet my inexplicable feelings for Suka linger. He still tugs at my senses, like a dream I don't want to wake from. The one good dream in my sea of nightmares.

I slide closer to him on the bench, a strange urge to rest my head on his shoulder overtaking me. And why should I fight it?

He turns abruptly as the longhouse door opens, relieving me of my foolish notion.

"Ref," he says.

My husband stands in the doorway, his stance wide. I take him in slowly, from his dark leather boots to his messy hair. Although most people rarely notice or acknowledge him, his presence alone is weighty. He does not dominate the room, like Gudrid's husband Thorfinn, nor does he make people feel anxious, like Helgi. He simply fills his space completely.

His voice is gruff, his eyes unswerving, as he stares Suka down. "What do you want?"

Tyr stands behind Ref, waiting to enter. My husband blocks the doorway, unruffled by the large warrior behind him.

The fire in the center of the room chokes out black smoke, its final bits of wood smoldering down to charred ash. I am trapped. This longhouse has no other door.

It would be easy enough for Ref to fall upon Suka and kill him right here. By all rights, he should. When I was recovering from the stillbirth of my son, Suka stepped into Ref's place and carried me deep into the woods, with no intention of returning me to camp. In his jealousy, Suka attacked Gudrid when she came to retrieve me, and he would have killed her, if not for her wolf's timely intervention.

I glance at his arm. Even now, scars run the length of it. I am sure his torso still bears witness to the wolf attack he survived.

But Ref will not be violent. Not without my permission.

Suka finally answers Ref's question. "We have made progress with the Skraelings. They have given Tyr one of their women for a wife." His eyes veer toward mine, their dark depths impenetrable. Did he, too, take a native wife?

He continues. "Their weapons are crude, and they revere our

swords since they have very little metal. They paint their bodies and homes with red ochre." A half-smile twists his lips. "Tyr refuses to coat himself with it, which is probably for the best. He would likely use their entire supply, the huge oaf."

Tyr finally pushes past Ref, grunting as he drops onto the bench opposite me. "My wife is pleasing. But I am Viking, not Skraeling." He beams a knowing smile at me, his blond hair catching sun rays from the hole in the roof.

"Indeed." Ref crosses his arms, waiting.

Before Suka can say another word, Valdis appears behind my husband, tapping Ref's shoulder with her talon-like fingernail. "My women and I need to weave."

I am sure they do. In one of their typical time-wasting activities, volva sit around and try to weave fate, like the three *norns* in our stories. I'd like to join them and weave them up a tapestry of doom. But I have no household skills.

I do have other skills, however. Atli probably waits for me to join him for swordplay. I push up from the bench and everything stills. The volva stare at me, positioned in an awkward line behind my husband. Ref's curious eyes fix on mine. Suka stands and offers me a short bow. I can almost hear everyone holding their breath.

I was born to lead.

"I am training my warrior today. Ref, please rejoin our crew as they stock the wood for winter. Suka and Tyr, you are welcome to sleep in the furthermost hut as long as you stay." As I pass by Ref, I brush his hand with mine.

Valdis doesn't give way for me to pass. I count four of her five women behind her.

She snaps her fingers in my face, her eyes dancing in some private exultation. Before I can move, her long-nailed hand rests on my stomach. "You'll be needing my Kitta soon, I imagine. Have you had any sickness?"

She knows.

I snatch her thin wrist, wrapping both my hands around it. I begin to wring her arm like a chicken's neck, but she doesn't cry out. Ref pretends not to notice and goes to sit across from Suka.

I speak under my breath. "I am not sick. But you will be if you mention this again."

She chokes out a laugh. "Dear Freydis. Always trying to blanket your own pain by bringing it to others. Your poor husband." Her eyes trail over to Ref. "Your poor *splendid* husband."

Before I can respond, she yanks her wrist from my grasp, throwing her arm to the sky as if she's praising her gods. She leads her women into the longhouse without looking back.

And this is her fatal flaw. She is so proud and fearless, she forgets to take in her surroundings. She forgets where her place is in this camp.

I will help her remember.

Outside, a solid gray-black cloud looms like a beached whale, mirroring my mood. Will Suka and Tyr stay? And for how long?

I cannot let Suka's presence distract me from my goal of gathering as many goods as possible before winter. I hate to overwinter here, but we have no choice. It is too late to sail back toward Greenland, where my brother sits snug and happy, the undisputed head of the family. When I return and prove my ability to provide for Brattahlid—to be more aggressive in acquiring wealth for our people—Leif will have no excuse for clinging to the farm. Besides, I will also return with many of Leif's slaves, and they will support me. I will take what I want most and spit in the face of the Fates.

As I follow a trickle of stream that widens into a rushing creek, my senses sharpen. Atli is close by, I am sure, but so is something or someone else. A slight movement shifts leaves on the forest floor near the open field we use for sparring.

Instinctively, I move toward the trees. I string my bow and nock an arrow. As I halt, a tawny coat catches my eye. Tracing it upward, I can make out forked horns. A stag.

My brothers never understood my innate hunting abilities. When I want to be stealthy, my presence goes undetected—not only by people, but also by prey. Thorstein joked that the animals didn't start because I hated to bathe and smelled like one of their own.

I creep close enough to take a shot and loose the arrow, pleased again to watch its sure flight. I stole these arrows from Leif before I sailed, knowing his blacksmith hammered the tips into the sharpest points in Greenland.

The struck stag leaps, then blindly tears toward me. Instead of running, as I should, a strange peace washes over me and I stand enthralled by its muscular power. Atli's shouts break into my trance.

"Freydis! Run!"

Before I can move, the panting stag tumbles into the grass nearby, its body stilling. I stare down into its darkening eyes as Atli shakes my shoulder.

"What were you doing? You could have been killed!" His blond hair tufts like cloud wisps around his face. Such a child's face, really. A child who could not possibly understand what the mushrooms have done to me.

I shake my head in an attempt to clear the webs of confusion that have taken up residence. "We will gut the stag before we spar."

Atli nods, pulling his knife as I pull mine. We work in silence. I suppose Gudrid would take this opportunity to speak to the boy, but I do not. I need no words to understand his ambition, his drive to become the best warrior.

For although every person must die, our reputations will not. Atli and I are yoked in our determination to be remembered throughout time.

FOUR

WE DRAG THE CARCASS back to camp, leaving it with my slave, Huld, for butchering. The old hag is quite possibly an even worse cook than I am, but she does her duty without slacking.

I chose two particularly old and ugly slave women for this voyage, knowing what kind of havoc beautiful young women can wreak on a crew of Viking men. It is questionable how well Valdis and her bunch of fresh young flowers will fare on the long voyage home. But perhaps Valdis shares the carnal standards of most volva, bringing her women along to ensure the men's pleasure.

As we amble back toward the field, I counsel Atli. "You must not shirk when you draw blood. Your first thought will be to draw back when you have struck someone. It is not the same as killing an animal."

The boy nods, his eyes serious. "I roped a dead boar from a tree limb for my sword practice. Though it stained my tunic and trousers, I think I am ready for blood."

"Clever. Who told you to do that?"

"Your husband, m'lady."

Sometimes I forget that Ref is also a swordsman, not merely a woodworker or a ship's hand.

Atli takes up his stance and I position myself nearby, unsheathing an older sword that has been dulled for sparring purposes. I have loaned him my father's helmet, which he carefully places on his head. I wear no helmet, but we both wear leather arm braces and vests for added protection.

As Atli takes up a shield in one hand, he draws his less-blunted sword, meeting my challenging gaze. His confidence has grown, which I am happy to see. An uncertain warrior is no warrior at all. I will not go easy on this young man.

I know he is experiencing the same rush of excitement I am: short breathing, sharp focus, and a shaking of the arms and hands that must be controlled before battle. I grip my weapon and give the word.

The boy rushes me, attempting a side attack with both sword and shield. I block it easily, knocking his aside and pushing my shield and sword forward in one movement. This would have been a fatal blow to his stomach, and he groans.

Charging again, he aims for my head. I block with my shield, cutting my blade sideways toward his exposed side.

He mounts a full attack, forcing me to retreat. I foolishly expose my sword hand, and he delivers a chop that would have removed my hand, had we been in battle.

"This is good!" I shout, proud of his small victory.

We continue sparring until we are both winded. As we drop our weapons, sinking into the soft grass, Ref approaches. He looks relaxed and happy, so perhaps Suka's visit has not distressed him as much as it has me.

He speaks to Atli. "I was watching you. Do not lower your sword and go for the legs when you could strike at the head. Otherwise you will be dead."

I know Ref's harsh words are born out of deep concern for the boy, but Atli does not see through his bluster as I do. He grimaces, refusing to acknowledge Ref's advice. I shove an elbow into his arm, inclining my head toward my husband.

He widens his eyes, gazing innocently at Ref. "Yes, of course, m'lord."

I grin. The boy does have spirit. Part of being a Viking warrior is knowing how to harness that driving anger. The other part is knowing when to release it, as the berserkers do.

Just as I did, when I killed Skraelings who attacked our camp at Straumsfjord.

I lean into Atli, my thin frame easily supported by his bulk. I shield my eyes from the sunlight reflecting off Ref's serious face.

"He will do fine, Ref. If he can fight me, he can fight anyone."

My husband leans down toward me, casting his features into shadow. "True. It is a rare father who trains his child as thoroughly as Eirik the Red has trained you." His voice is charged with sadness I have not noticed before. Does he wish I had never trained to fight? That I would stay home like his mother and sisters, cooking and weaving and waving men off on their voyages?

I feel my nostrils flare and I jump to my feet, nearly toppling Ref. I brush past him. "It appears I have other pressing chores to attend to, like…salting the meat. Carry my sword and shield when you come back to the longhouse."

Ref gives me a confused look but I stalk off, not glancing back.

He basically insulted my upbringing, which in turn means he doesn't approve of my entire life. Maybe he didn't even want to sail to Vinland, although he never said otherwise.

Marriage is a difficult thing.

We choke down one of Huld's nearly inedible meals in the longhouse, still uncomfortably close to Finnbogi and Helgi's crew. Maybe I should allow a few of my men to help the Icelanders chop trees for their new longhouse. Our separation cannot happen soon enough.

Tyr and Suka are deep in conversation with Ref. Perhaps my husband will befriend them, which would be helpful. My crew is loyal enough, but loyal to me. My husband needs someone to trust, to talk to. I cannot be that companion when I am making decisions for all of us here in Vinland.

Valdis tries to catch my eye, again. I have sensed her icy stare all evening. As she swept into the room, I noticed she was dressed finely, in a bold blue dress with a fox-fur cape. But I have not looked at her since.

As Huld awkwardly hands me a charred hunk of bread, I snatch a glance at Valdis. Her white hair is twisted and coiled around a golden headpiece, not so very unlike a crown. She has used charcoal to rim her eyes. When she abruptly stops talking to stare at me, I gasp. Although I am sure men might find the pale green of her eyes more noticeable lined in black, to me those eyes look like caverns leading to deepest Helheim.

Smiling slowly, she leans in toward her husband and whispers in his ear. Finnbogi clears his throat and begins to speak, his voice slowly drowning out the other conversations in the large room.

"As a sign of good faith, my wife would like to ask that your crew join ours for wine and dancing." Finnbogi nods at one of Valdis' hovering women, who takes his glass and dips it into a barrel. Deep red wine sparkles in the firelight. My crew gasps. Wine is not easy to come by.

Finnbogi smiles. "We are glad to share this wine from Norway, in anticipation of the grapes we have found here in Vinland. When the sun warms the earth again, we will dig up the roots for trading. Will you join us in our reveling?"

Irritation crawls up my throat like a scratching bug. I nearly choke trying to swallow the half-chewed bite of deer meat in my mouth. I don't want to revel with the Icelanders. I don't want to share the grapevines from Vinland with them, either.

Suka leans over, giving me an intense look from his end of the table. I am not sure what it means. He clarifies by placing one finger to his lips. He wants me to stay quiet, but as leader, I should be the one to respond to Finnbogi's request.

Before I can speak, Suka oversteps his bounds and answers. "Perhaps we could also gather around the fire and tell stories? I am sure with all these Vikings gathered, we have some rich tales."

I remain silent, doubting the wisdom of both crews drinking and mingling this night, so soon after my fight with Finnbogi. Ref's eyes meet mine, but I cannot guess his thoughts.

Once again, my husband is completely useless when it comes to decision-making.

"Share the wine," I command. "We will make merry tonight."

Warmth has crawled up into my hair and made me smile when I should be hateful. It does not distress me that I sit on the dirt floor instead of in a chair, like Valdis, who sits gloriously with her furs wrapped about her neck and her amber staff glinting in the firelight. Her women curl up at her feet, tired from their dancing. I did not join in, nor did Ref or Suka.

The dark-haired girl called Kitta stares at me, though not in a hostile way. She seems observant and curious. Valdis suggested Kitta has some experience with birthing. Perhaps I will talk with the girl, try to win her to my side.

Ref and Tyr walk away from our loud group, into the moonlit darkness. I know they will pace a circle around the camp several times over. At Straumsfjord, Thorfinn had his men build a log wall to protect us. Here, we are not as close to the sea, but it is wise to keep a watch. I shudder, remembering the time a Skraeling woman silently infiltrated our camp. Gudrid kept her head and tried to trade with the woman, instead of killing her, as I would have. This was wise, as it gave us time to prepare for their next visit…which was an attack.

Two of our men and one of their women have already told tales, mostly of the exploits of gods and goddesses. Each storyteller wants to outdo the other, fueled by wine and pride.

"I come from the Swede land, where the god Frey was buried. We have many sacred mounds," one of their blond-haired men says.

Huld croaks out, "Frey is nothing in comparison to his sister, Freyja. She is perfect in beauty and clever, a favorite of the gods. I once saw her cat carriage in the sky."

Suka's voice slides into the air, tinged with a hint of warning. "Why should we fear dead gods? It is wiser to fear the warriors in our midst. Tyr was guard to the Norwegian king. Freydis is a Skraeling-slayer."

His dark eyes slide to me. Though his words are simple, his underlying tone ripples with respect. He is trying to frighten the Icelanders.

I am surprised by his words, and not only because Suka himself would be considered a Skraeling in Greenland. It is because he knows what happened right after I killed those Skraelings—I lost my child, then very nearly lost my mind. I was no warrior then.

I hold his eyes, unable to hold back a pleased smile.

"Come and sit by me, warrior-woman." Valdis' light voice carries a thinly-veiled edge. She motions me to the now-empty seat at her side. Her husband and his brother have left the longhouse, probably retreating to their hut. They must be sleepy after their day's work felling trees for their new camp.

What game is Valdis playing? Most of the time she only acknowledges my presence with her knife-like words.

Again, I wish Gudrid were here—she would tell me the right thing to do. Her wisdom is indisputable, and has steered me right many times. Most would say it is because she is a trained volva, gifted with foresight, but that is not why. Now she has turned Christian, she does not practice the pagan ways or recite their chants. Instead, she talks to her Christian god as if he were walking alongside her, like a friend. This seems to give her insight others do not have.

I glance around, wondering who my true friends are in this camp.

Atli, surely. My warrior-boy lounges near the youngest woman from Valdis' bunch. I recognize her as the blonde girl who bumped her hip into Atli earlier. Now she has taken off her brooches, letting her overdress slide down to reveal the sheer linen shift beneath. This is ill-advised, but it does not surprise me at all. I am pleased to see Atli turn his face from her enticement to meet my gaze. He has not yet drunk enough to dull him in a fight.

Suka, too, watches to see what I decide. I shake off my stupor and stand without swaying. It takes some effort to avoid smashing into men's hands or legs as they recline by the blazing fire, but I succeed in making it to Valdis' side.

Dropping stiffly into the carved chair, I turn toward the witch. Her dancing eyes skim my face and her lips arch into a proud sneer.

Two things I can see clearly: I can give no ground to the Icelanders, no matter how generous they seem with their supplies, and there will never be a reconciliation between us.

FIVE

LIKE SALMON THAT HAVE tired themselves in their mad rush to spawn, men and women slip back toward their huts, exhausted. Valdis has not spoken a word to me, nor has she met my eyes since I first sat next to her.

My own eyelids are drooping, but I refuse to give up my chair until Valdis abandons hers.

She finally stands, with the air of one who has more pressing affairs to attend to. Suka scrambles up from his place on the floor, dusting off his woolen trousers. My husband and Tyr have not returned, perhaps swapping stories themselves as they patrol.

As Valdis glides past Suka, she whispers into his ear, observing me from the corner of her eyes. Suka's face remains unmoved as a calm sea, although I suspect she has told him some bold lie about me.

When the young blonde girl openly kisses Atli's lips before sailing out behind her leader, I hold back a groan. It is clear that Valdis has brought these women along to make inroads with our men.

Atli obviously isn't excited about her attentions, because he crawls onto the built-in bench that runs the length of the longhouse, ready for sleep. A few of my other crewmen snore on benches.

Suka takes my hand, pulling me closer to the waning firelight. "We sat outside by the blazing fire once; do you remember?"

Thankfully, that night is one I can recall. Suka had given me his cloak to ward off the chill as he sat next to me. I felt full with child and invincible. Yet perhaps even then, my baby boy was dead inside me.

"Freydis?"

I shake my head to break my daze. My child is buried in the forest at Straumsfjord. Perhaps I should go to him.

I lightly squeeze Suka's hand. "How long would it take to sail to Straumsfjord?"

He shakes his head. "It is a long journey, and there are too many Skraelings there. They have taken our old camp."

My stomach churns at the thought of Skraelings finding my boy's grave, perhaps digging up his tiny body. I drop my face to my raised knees, hair tumbling around me like a heavy veil. Suka pushes my curls behind my ear, exposing the side of my face. Glancing up at him, I take in the slant of his dark eyes that are fringed in kohl lashes, his gold-tan skin, and his unique earthy smell. With his pure native Greenlandic blood, he is so different from us and so captivating. It is good he has found a home here, so he can be free from Leif's slavery.

He rightly guesses my unspoken fear. "The Skraelings are superstitious. They will not dig up a grave."

The fire sputters, sending up a puff of smoke that doesn't escape from the ceiling hole as it should. I shove the metal rod in it, stirring up the embers, and Suka places small logs on it. It is hard for me to stay silent for long, so I ask what I need to know.

"What did Valdis want from you?"

He stares at the flames that quickly bite into the dried wood. "You need to stay away from that woman, Freydis."

I won't be put off. "But what did she say?"

Before he can answer, Ref opens the longhouse door. The door is ornate—white pine he carved himself to replace the flimsy piece Leif's men had used when they built the camp. He cautiously steps toward the fire, unable to make out if anyone is on the floor.

Turning back to Suka, I whisper. "So?"

"We will speak tomorrow," he whispers, releasing my hand before standing and greeting my husband. "Ref. Is Tyr with you?"

My husband's sure voice fills the space between us. "He is back at your hut. Thorgrim guards our camp now." Stepping up to the fire, he warms his hands.

One of these men is the father of the child I carry. I try not to measure Ref against Suka, but it is difficult. Ref is shorter, and older. Suka has always seemed full of passion, from his ability to run fleet-footed as a deer to his unshakeable interest in my life.

If only I could recall if his interest ever led to something physical, back at the forest in Straumsfjord. I should just ask him if he...if we...

Ref looks down at me, taking my arm and gently helping me to my feet. Why is my first impulse to pull away? Why does my husband always annoy, instead of enchant me? I know women can love their husbands. Gudrid certainly loves hers, although I can't resist teasing her about the men who fall in love with her—my brother Leif, in particular. That manly brute goes positively witless around her.

Suka gives me one last nod, then slips out into the night. Ref and I stand in an uncomfortable silence I don't know how to fill. His hand slides from my arm to my waist, where it lingers. Can he feel how my stomach already widens? I seem to be growing faster with this child.

His eyes meet mine in the firelight, his green eye glinting gold, his blue eye bright. Such strange, wonderful eyes. What does he see when he looks at me?

His deep voice cracks as he speaks. "I saw Valdis and her women, gathered in the small grove outside our camp."

It is unlike my husband to offer information like this. Something must have seemed significant about this encounter with the volva. I sigh. Why can't he just say what he means?

"And what were they doing there, Ref?"

He motions to the door, obviously ready to return to our hut. I shadow him closely as we step out into the moonlight and follow the dirt path.

He finally answers. "I don't know. They had lanterns in a circle around a large stone. They were chanting."

I stop, kicking at a rock that pushed into my leather boot. "That's all those volva ever do."

He nods in silence. His gray-and-white hair glints in the moonlight.

"Well? Was there something else?" It seems I must prod things out of him.

He unlocks the door of our hut with the key dangling on his belt. He steps inside, then rustles into a bag of pinecones, preparing to start a fire.

Sparks from his flint stone shower onto the pinecones and coals beneath, finally catching into a small burn. He shuffles to the side of the hut, preparing to undress.

Why am I standing here, watching my husband do all this? Because he has not answered my question.

I put my hands on my hips. "Are you deaf now, like your sister's dog?"

He jerks his head up. "No."

"Then why did you not answer? I asked what else those vexing women were doing in the grove."

His eyes crinkle in a smile, and I realize he is drawing this out so he can keep my attention. I feel flattered, but at the same time, annoyed.

He continues to smirk as he begins to remove his tunic. I stamp to his side and yank it over his head, nearly ripping a sleeve off. My scowl meets his surprised smile.

Laughing, he sinks into his favorite chair, pulling me down onto his lap. He nuzzles at my neck. "I will tell you if you tell me this: do I need to make Suka leave camp?"

Does he sense how I feel toward Suka? Do his words hold an undercurrent of jealousy? Or is he in earnest, afraid Suka's presence disturbs me after he tried to fight with Gudrid at Straumsfjord? Perhaps he thinks Suka will sow discord in this camp as well?

His face betrays nothing of his emotions. This is what I love and hate about my husband: his ability to tamp down anger and rage and desire. I have to give vent to mine, or it is possible I will burst into flames, from the ends of my bony toes to the springing coils of my hair.

I try to remain calm as I answer. "Of course Suka should remain here as long as he likes. What is he to me? I do not care that he is my brother's runaway slave. Leif can come over and retrieve his own property."

Ref cups my cheeks with his rough hands. In his slow, demanding way, he pulls my face down to his, catching my lips in a nearly savage kiss.

When he releases me, I gasp for air, the slight taste of blood in my mouth.

Satisfied, he pushes me up and strides over to the bed. "I will tell you what I saw. There was a body on that stone, Freydis. A sacrifice."

Shocking as Ref's statement is, the wine seems to have stolen my alertness and hindered my movements. I crawl next to him on the bed, prepared to ask questions, but I fall into a hard sleep instead.

SIX

SUNLIGHT POURS THROUGH THE window, warming my bed. Ref has also stoked a fire for me before going out to work, so I feel snug as a rabbit in its hole. I have a strong desire for one of Gudrid's herbal teas this morning, probably to shake off my heavy head from the wine I indulged in last night. Did Ref really tell me Valdis offered a human sacrifice?

Dagmar, my slave that is even older than Huld, pushes my door open, pulling me from my bleak thoughts. Her coarse white hairs are close-cropped, yet they still manage to protrude in every direction. Ref must have forgotten to lock the door. What was he thinking, in a divided camp like ours?

"Would you be wanting a washing, m'lady?"

I laugh outright, knowing the woman has mostly worked in the fields over the years, not in the house. "Just how many washings have you done for ladies, Dagmar?"

She drops her head. "None, m'lady."

"Then why begin now? We have set up camp in a strange land. Shall we act as if we are royalty in Norway, like all my brother's wealthy friends? I can clean myself perfectly well."

Her back hunched, Dagmar slowly begins to shuffle out the door. Unexpected remorse fills me. "I thank you for your concern, though. You have shown admirable loyalty." Her eyes brighten at this.

As I close the door behind her, I wonder if she was hinting that I needed to bathe. I find my horse chestnut soap and clean myself with wet rags as I plan what I will accomplish today. I cannot abide being stuck in our hut for long.

Atli will be working with some of our men, helping the Icelanders fell trees. Ref will lead the rest of our crew as they chop wood, storing it up for winter and for trade in Greenland. I am sure the volva will sleep later and laze about the longhouse, useless as they are.

Because my feet are constantly cold, no matter what the weather, I slip into my leather boots lined with seal-hide. Hunger clenches my stomach tight, nearly forcing me to a chair. I always forget to eat, but I must take something for this babe inside me.

In one of Ref's carved boxes, I find deer jerky and smoked trout. I eat quickly, then sheathe my curved knife on my belt. For a larger weapon, I waver between my sword and my bow, but finally decide on my sword.

Although the Skraelings have not yet visited us in Vinland, I know they might. It was a Skraeling arrow that killed my favorite brother, Thorvald, in this land. He was hastily buried before the crew abandoned camp, and I still have not found his grave. His memory tears at me as I prepare to go out today.

As I lock the door with my own belt key, Thorgrim steps around me on the path. He begins to hum, in a creaking, lusty fashion, then dips his head to me. Suddenly I'm aware that I, too, was humming loudly. I must do this without thinking, probably to feel less alone when I venture out.

But as I slip into the grove, I silence my hums. Today I am going to uncover what Valdis and her women have been doing.

The tight birch trees that line the cleared grove have turned vibrant yellow. I walk up to one and break off a twig to inhale its faint minty scent. Smaller than the pines and spruce the men take for building, these birches will provide nice firewood for us. I touch the tree's peeling bark, giving a silent thanks to it.

It is a habit I have—talking to wood. Whether it's the boards of my ship's deck, or the trees of the forest, I feel an urge to speak to this life-giving resource. To thank it for giving of itself for us.

When I was a child, my father would laugh and tease as I touched the ship's planks almost reverently. But my father stopped laughing when he saw me climb the ship's mast, all the way to the top. He stopped laughing when he realized how I could sense the weather coming by the way the ship handled. He stopped laughing when the arrows I made flew faster and farther than any man's.

I move into a clearing, where a rough-edged stone dominates the deep center of the grove. I stalk around it, noticing the tamped-down leaves from last night's ritual. Perhaps Ref saw something more last night, but I wasn't alert enough to ask him the right questions.

It would be hard to discern bloodstains against the smoke-colored rock, but I discover a few darker streaks in its crevices. It is almost as if the volva scrubbed the stone clean, which would explain the lack of staining if they sacrificed something larger, like an animal...or a person.

Tracking around the stone, I search for remains of a fire, or even for charred bones. The women would probably try to hide the body of their victim. Human sacrifice is not so readily accepted in Viking circles, now that Christianity has come to Iceland and Greenland.

Nothing looks disturbed except a circle of holes that the lantern stakes left behind. I am missing something, I can feel it. Something I need to find.

Sometimes, the best way to see things clearly is to force yourself to take a different view. And for me, that usually means a higher view. I tuck my sword into a tree crevice, then find a low-branched birch next to the circle. Grabbing a lower limb, I climb until the top limbs dwindle and weaken.

The light sway of the tree makes me feel powerful, invulnerable. Like the goddess Freyja herself, one with the earth and sky. I amuse myself by watching a turtle-shaped cloud creep by, seemingly close enough to touch.

But the sun has shifted, and I must be quick about things, before the mid-day meal is served. If I am missing, surely Ref will worry.

Gazing down into the circle that is blanketed with yellow leaves, I make myself fully aware. My senses begin to throb and shiver, ready to come to my aid.

I take in the area, first as a whole, and then bit by bit. A squirrel chirps at me from his nearby tree, angry that I have invaded his world. Several hawks swoop over the grove. Nothing moves on the forest floor, but my roving eyes stop, fixing on a sideways tuft of grass.

A chill passes through my body and I lock my legs closer to the tree, but I can see no one around. I begin to pick my way back down the tree, more carefully than I climbed up. I am, after all, with child. Gudrid would scold me roundly if she saw what I just did.

After I drop to the ground, I snatch up my sword and walk to the misplaced grass. When I poke at it, I find it shifts easily, tumbling aside like it was placed there.

And someone surely has placed it, because under the crumbling dirt, in a shallow-dug hole, is a severed head.

SEVEN

BEFORE I CAN CONTAIN my horror, there is a movement behind me. I pitch myself into the undergrowth, remembering to fall on the side that does not bear my sheathed sword.

Lying in silence, I wait for another noise, but hear nothing. My stillness does not last long, because the babe rears its head against the injustice of my tossing it about, and I am forced to empty my stomach on the leaves.

I know it is not merely the babe causing this. My stomach heaves again and I retch, envisioning the smashed face in the hole. It is almost as if chunks of flesh were missing from it. I can't be certain, but it did not look like any of our crew members. Where did they find this unfortunate person?

Although I have grown up killing and gutting animals, I cannot stay near my grisly find. I stumble back toward the longhouse, making several other stops to vomit.

The camp seems empty as I struggle to unlock my door. A man's voice sounds behind me and I jump, still connected to the door by the key on my belt.

"What is wrong?"

I turn to recognize Finnbogi, his white-blond beard trimmed short, far closer than Helgi trims his. Has he been following me? Surely the Icelandic leader has some better use for his time.

I take a deep, steadying breath, not only for me, but hopefully for the babe. I imagine scents I enjoy, like cedar and cumin. Gathering my wits, I react as I normally would—with annoyance.

"Why should you assume something is wrong with me just because I struggle with my lock? Perhaps you think I am weak?"

His hazel eyes narrow, giving me another way to mark the difference between him and his brother. I have noticed Helgi's eyes are pale blue. It is important I discern between them, because Helgi is by far the more aggressive of the two.

"Many apologies for asking, Freydis." He whirls on his high leather boot and stalks off toward his hut.

I return to the lock, inwardly cursing it for being so difficult. I will have Ref change it out, because I am sure he has brought others.

A damp chill has penetrated our hut's crumbling mud chinking. I am reminded that Leif designed this Vinland camp to be temporary. Taking my brown wool cape from its peg, I pull its wide, fur-lined hood over my head. I unstrap my sword and sheath, dropping them on the bed. My stomach continues to lurch, and for once, I wish Dagmar would return and offer me food. My desire for a hot herbal drink has only grown stronger as my stomach has grown emptier.

But there is no use standing about, wishing for things. I shall go into the longhouse and prepare my own tea.

As I approach the longhouse door, heated women's voices drift from the windows in the back. I creep toward the window opening and hunch below it so I can hear more.

"...it is not what I expected," a younger voice says.

"You left your expectations behind in Iceland when you chose the path of the volva." Valdis' light voice holds a mirthless undertone. "You belong to our family now."

A too-eager voice responds. "And we will be the strongest family in Vinland. Kitta, do not be foolish."

Kitta, the one who must have questioned Valdis, murmurs something. Valdis cuts her off. "Vinland is not the only land we will rule. As everyone in Greenland knows, Leif has a weakness for women. *Blonde* women, most of all." She says this in an intimate way, causing the others to laugh.

I swallow, hoping to tamp down the dry heaves that threaten to gag me. Much as I despise my brother, I will never see him taken advantage of by these volva. Do they have evil intentions for Brattahlid?

I have heard enough. I creep back to the door, then stand and carelessly shove it open. Stalking inside, I grab a cup from a shelf and use it to dip hot water from the pot.

The volva in the back have fallen silent. My old wenches are nowhere to be seen. Lazy hags. They should have been listening so they could inform me of the Icelanders' conversations.

It is not my nature to pretend things are cheerful when they are not. It is far easier to shout about my betrayals and my losses. But today I will remain silent, allowing my own knowledge to grow more powerful.

Valdis glides closer, her full skirts lapping around her heels like water. Today she wears an embroidered light green overdress, fastened by silver brooches that are carved with twining snakes. Very fitting.

I force a smile. "And what are the volva working on today?"

Valdis yawns rudely. "My husband's wine was so plenteous, we had to sleep later this morning. But you must be tired as well, talking to your Skraeling so late into the night."

Even as heat rises to my face, I determine to dull the stabbing point of her words. "Indeed, I was. But I have always woken early and worked hard, no matter how much wine I imbibe."

The other women scurry around, preparing food and pretending not to listen. Everyone except Kitta, who watches us openly. She is pulling away from her leader, which might be a very dangerous thing.

Rummaging through the herb chest, I take a handful of mint leaves and several small flowers that resemble what Gudrid uses for teas. I dump out my lukewarm water on the dirt floor, which throws mud onto Valdis' skirt. Taking fresh hot water from the pot, I drop my herbs into it.

Unsheathing my knife, I set it on the table before settling into Valdis' preferred carved chair. I meet her challenging glare with a deliberate smile before I begin to sip my tea.

After forcing myself to drink my strange brew, I sit until the men come inside for their mid-day meal. Dagmar and Huld drag into the longhouse, wet from washing clothing in the creek. Perhaps they are not so lazy after all. They flap around me like hens, scolding when they discover parsley in my cup.

"Could make you lose the babe, m'lady." Dagmar shakes her head, shocked at my ignorance. So my servants know of the baby, as well.

And what if Ref asks me outright if I am with child? Soon enough he will notice my rounded stomach. I watch him now as he speaks with Tyr, using his finger to carve invisible designs on the table. I know what my husband will do if I tell him we are having a babe. He will carve toys and a cradle. Perhaps a sword, in hopes of a boy.

But any daughter of mine will learn to use weapons too.

I let my gaze trail over the room. Suka is missing. I motion to Atli as one of Valdis' women places another bowl of stew by my elbow. I hesitate to eat it, wondering if Valdis would dare poison me in front of my men. But the thick stew is made with my favorite fish—trout—and I cannot resist.

Atli settles at my side, his thick blond hair pulled back into a band. He smells of the sweat of hard labor and his powerful drive seems to charge the air around him. My brothers were also like this at his age. No wonder the volva gape at him.

"Where is Suka?" I ask.

Atli shrugs. "I have not seen him this day. He did not come to the forest with our men. Perhaps he still sleeps?"

Suka may not enjoy working with our Viking crew, but it is unlike him to miss the meal. He promised we would speak today. Why has he not looked for me?

My neck hairs crawl as an idea overtakes me. No. It could not be possible. Yet I did observe that the disembodied head had thick, dark brows. Tan skin. I could not tell if it was a man or woman.

It could not be Suka. Surely he left the longhouse after my husband saw the volva performing their sacrificial ceremony.

Didn't he?

EIGHT

MY SPOON CLATTERS INTO the bowl and I jump from my seat, stumbling toward the door. Atli comes alongside me. Valdis mutters something about the "mother's illness", but it only spurs me onward. I do not believe the soup has made me sick, but my fear has.

We continue past my hut, on toward the edge of camp. I gather strength as I move, shaking off Atli's help and breaking into a run. Suka's door has no lock, so I burst into the small, dark hut.

The room is bare, save for one ponderous war hammer that I recognize as Tyr's.

Suka is gone.

I turn in a slow circle on the packed dirt floor, unable to comprehend where Suka would go, and why he would go alone. Did he meet the volva late last night? Perhaps Valdis had whispered a time and place to him? Was it his head in the hole?

My sight blurs a bit at the edges, a problem I have had since I ate the berserker mushrooms. Atli's strong, wide hand grasps my arm.

"You need to sit down, m'lady." He guides me to one of the makeshift beds, and I sink into it, hating my weakness. Part of me wants to call Ref here, so he can see that Suka has vanished. But the more powerful side of me prevails, as it always does.

"I am hardy enough. Go back to the longhouse and behave as if nothing has happened. Meet me at dusk in our sparring field, for I have something to teach you in that light."

Atli gives a stiff nod and slowly steps outside. He knows better than to cross me when my mind is made up, even if I am weakened.

I lie back on the wool blanket, which smells decidedly of a man's sweat. It is a familiar scent to me, since I grew up the only daughter in a house-full of men. The smell seems to be the cure I needed, as my mind and vision begin to clear. I prop myself up on one elbow, waiting a moment. When the room does not fade from view, I sit up a bit more. No reason to lie about when I need to track Suka, to be sure he is still alive.

I take my curved knife from its leather sheath, lightly running my finger along its edge. A satisfying sliver of blood trickles down my finger, so I know the blade is sharp enough to slit the throat of any volva who stands in my way.

I will return to the grove, to examine the head that was so carelessly buried there. To be sure it is not Suka's. Perhaps I will find the body, as well.

A light rap sounds on the door. Maybe Ref has followed me here.

"Open," I say.

A woman in a green velvet cape steps into the room. As she pulls her hood down, wavy black hair tumbles about her shoulders. Milky white skin sets off the gentle sky blue eyes that fix on me.

Kitta speaks. "Are you well?"

I am sure Valdis has sent her to inform on me. I will not give her the satisfaction of knowing I have struggled today.

"Of course."

Her eyes travel from the unkempt bed to my slumped back. I straighten and force myself to stand.

Kitta rushes to my side, carefully wrapping an arm around my waist. I meet her eyes and a rush of familiarity passes over me. I have seen that look before. Firm, yet loving. Filled with concern, yet determined.

Kitta is a healer, like Gudrid. I can almost feel her strength flowing into me.

She speaks as we move toward the door. "Where are you going, Freydis?"

"Into the forest." She does not need to know the truth.

She places her other hand on my waist, turning me toward her. I am forced to meet her eyes.

"You have been to the grove." Those eyes study my face, probing into my very thoughts, it seems.

I feel powerless to lie again. "Yes."

She sighs. "Of course you would have to do that."

I recoil at her harshness. "And what is wrong with knowing what goes on in my own camp?"

"You are in danger, though perhaps you count it lightly," she continues. "It is wise to tread cautiously, but I know this is not your way."

I shove my palm into her shoulder. Like most women, she is shorter than I am. I could knock her down and kill her right here.

Her eyes widen, but she doesn't step back. "I am not against you, Freydis. In truth, I came to warn you. If you will let me join your camp, I will leave the volva forever. But I must have your protection."

Her words warm me. She can see that I am in charge of my camp, and the safety of those in it. She believes I am more powerful than the volva.

I make a hasty decision, my words of reassurance rushing out. "Yes. Join us and you will be safe. We will tell Valdis I need you close, in case the baby comes early as it did last time."

"You have given birth before?"

I do not want to speak of it, but I must. "He was born dead. Too early." I try to explain, to convince myself as much as Kitta that this time it will be different. "This babe must be healthy. I have not had the same shooting pains, and it is bigger already."

She stretches her hand out, letting it hover over my stomach. Her short fingernails are a contrast to Valdis' talons. "May I?"

I nod. She lays her hand on my stomach, pressing in a circular motion. Although the babe has not moved yet, I feel a strange peace that this child will survive. I am further comforted when she nods.

"I have trained with my mother since I was a child. She has aided many women on their birth-beds. We will be certain when the babe kicks you, but I do feel this child is strong."

My responding smile wilts as I recall Gudrid speaking similar encouraging words to me before my stillbirth. It is probably the way of midwives from ages past, to whisper smooth words of hope to mothers.

"Let us speak no more of my baby today," I say. "You will come to my hut and tell me about the ceremony in the grove."

NINE

AS WE SETTLE IN my hut, I allow Kitta to sit in Ref's chair. She fingers the carved seals and whales along the sides. She has paled considerably, probably because of what she is about to recount to me. I sit on the end of the bed, hands firmly at my sides to keep me steady.

Her eyes travel to the fire, where a pinecone crackles, then burns down to embers. It has warmed outside, so I do not add more wood.

I try to prod her to speak by telling her what I already know. "Valdis has beheaded someone."

The girl nods, her innocent eyes brimming with unshed tears. Is she as guileless as she seems? Perhaps I am wrong to trust her. Perhaps she will carry stories about me back to Valdis.

"How old are you?" I ask abruptly.

"I am a full nineteen years." She takes in my face, perceiving my misgivings about her value to our camp. "I am no child. I can be of use to you." Her chin juts out, defiant.

She is older than she looks. When I was her age, I had seen many men killed and I had killed some myself. I must know Valdis' secrets, if I am to have an advantage over her, so I cannot relent in my questioning.

I prod her again. "I don't have all day, girl. Tell me."

She stretches her hands to the fire, soaking in the trifling warmth. "My mother wanted me to become a volva to help others. To bring words of hope to many villages, as our volva did. And then Valdis came to our village, full of otherworldly grandeur, and she said the gods had chosen me as volva. She said my child-birthing skills would help many."

Her voice grows stronger with each word she speaks. "And yet she cared nothing for my skills. She only wanted me for my body, so she could offer someone younger and fresher for the men."

My stomach turns. "She gave you to men?"

Kitta nods. "In each village we visited. They would bring offerings—furs, jewels, gold. She reveled in it. In return, she would speak the future. Finally, to win favor with the younger landowners, she would arrange for me to meet them during the night."

Color rushes to her cheeks, turning them scarlet. "The others gladly followed her on this voyage. But I wanted nothing more than to return to my family. She said I had to serve for four more years, to fulfill my parents' agreement. Otherwise I would bring shame on my family, and she would curse our family farm. Also, she would predict my death-day."

I exhale into a growl. "She couldn't curse a dog, much less speak the day you will die."

Kitta cowers deep into the chair, as no grown woman should. "Do not make light of her powers. I have seen them."

"Seen what? Stars falling from the skies? The ground opening up?

The dead brought back to life?"

Instead of laughing, she remains reflective. "Something like that. I have seen ghosts. She called them up in the peace-grove, before she sacrificed."

I lean forward, eager to understand. "What else did she do before she sacrificed?"

Her gaze moves back to the flames. "She brought her silver stool to stand on. She always uses it when she prepares a sacrifice. From the leather pouch on her belt, she removed special seeds and threw them onto the fire. Then she called to Odin. That is when I saw the ghosts. I was flying…or they were flying…and then Valdis had two of the volva, Birsa and Thorni, bring the woman forth from the trees."

I could shout with relief. "The *woman*, you say?"

She nods. "Yes, a Skraeling woman. She was not awake. Thorni and Fastni dragged the woman by the hair toward the stone, then Gilla picked up the Skraeling's feet. They hoisted her onto the rock. Valdis led a chant, and then handed Birsa her long carved axe."

Kitta stops speaking. I know she has seen horrors, but she must explain this death to me, an unjust death in my brother's camp. "Tell me quickly, then we will put it behind us. I do not hold you accountable for this," I add.

A thin wail escapes her lips. "By the gods, I watched. I was part of it, sure as any. I am doomed."

I move to her side, smoothing back her soft hair as if she were my own child. "I will not accuse you of this great evil. In fact, I swear to you, this death will be avenged. And not in the afterlife."

Her wide eyes rove my face, searching for proof of my threat. She must find what she is looking for, because she continues, her words clipped.

"Birsa tried to cut off the head. It did not work. Valdis took the axe and finished the job herself. Then she…the wand…she took the flesh. The flesh from the Skraeling's face. She ate it."

I swallow repeatedly, trying to choke down the bile that rises in my throat. The babe makes my stomach weak, and I have to clench my fists to keep from running to the waste bucket to vomit yet again.

Kitta finishes the sickening tale, her face blanched. "She forced the others to partake, saying we would draw strength from the Skraelings by taking this woman's body into ours. She said Odin had spoken through her weaving, promising that the volva would become sole rulers of this new land, and that this was how we had to bring about our fate." Tears rush down Kitta's face and she gasps between sobs. "I did not eat. I could not. Instead, I went closer to the fire, pretending the smoke from the burning seeds overwhelmed me. I ran to the edge of the circle and fell on the ground."

I wipe my mouth with a cloth and then go to sit at the girl's feet. "You have just told me that all the volva, except for you, joined in this…slaying?"

As if sensing a trap, she restates things. "I was not part of it." Her warm tears splash on my legs. "I cannot go back to her!"

I place a hand on her knee. "And you will not. You say there was only the one Skraeling? No others were killed?"

"I cannot say. There was more chanting, but I could not watch. I crept away into the dark. I joined your slave women in their hut, because I could not return to Valdis. You can ask them if you need surety."

I will do so, to verify her words, but not now, when Suka is missing. Now I must return to the grove and be sure the volva have killed no others.

TEN

SLIPPING OUT AS KITTA dissolves into a fit of weeping, I check the longhouse to make sure the volva are there before I return to their birch grove.

Once again, voices carry out the window before I get close.

A younger voice says, "She never came back last night. And today she acted strangely when we prepared the meal."

The others begin to murmur in agreement, but they fall silent when Valdis' voice cuts into the room, probably from her position in her favorite carved chair. "I see she is drawn to Freydis Eiriksdottir. It is natural she would want to help with the childbirth, since that is what she was trained for. If anyone could soften that copper-haired fox's demeanor, it would be Kitta. We will leave her in peace."

One anxious voice protests. "Perhaps you should tap her cheek three times with your amber staff, so she will forget our ceremony. If she were to tell anyone…"

Valdis laughs—an echoing, ghostly sound. "Soon enough it will not matter. Weave, my volva, spin and weave the fates of Freydis' men. I myself will knot the threads of her life and fetter her to the ones she hates most."

Immediately, I think of Leif. Or Valdis herself. Which enemy do I hate most?

To pull myself back from believing Valdis' magical words, I touch my knife's blade, wincing at its sharp nip on my finger. Is she burning her witch seeds in our longhouse? I feel strangely weak.

I whirl around, bolting toward the grove while I have sense to do so. I must pass by my men, who have moved closer to camp so they can split the logs and cart them to our huts. I consider hiding behind trees to avoid speaking to them, but decide against it. I will walk boldly, because I answer to no one.

I notice several Icelanders have joined my men, and I don't like it. I point to them as I walk by. "You there! And you. Yes, I speak to you. Go back to your own crew."

Ref splits his short log in one blow, then stares at me. He shakes his head. How dare he?

I stamp my foot to give weight to my words, although I am carrying no sword. Surely they would not attack me in front of my crew. "I said go now."

The Icelanders snarl and spit, but take up their axes and stride off into the forest. It is for the best. I don't want them reporting on my movements to Valdis. Ref shifts on his feet, as if he wants to speak to me, but instead he props another log on his tree stump, then drives his axe straight through. I turn my head at his show of silent fury, stalking off along the path toward the grove.

Thorgrim stands on the outskirts, halting me as I pass. "I will keep a watch for them. They will not join us again."

I ask him what I could not lower myself to ask Ref, after my abrupt command to the Icelanders. "Why were they here?"

His impassive eyes are shadowed by dark, unruly brows. "I believe it was three for three, m'lady. Three of their men joined us to chop wood, while three of ours went to help them fell trees. A show of good faith as we worked together."

And I just sent them back to their own crew.

That is unfortunate.

My brown cape and dull green overdress blend in seamlessly with the forest trees. But my hair does not, because most of the red-leaved trees have not changed yet. I drape the hood over my head and hasten toward the grove.

As I approach the loosened turf, a sense of foreboding sends a shudder through me. The chunk of grass has been moved. When I prod it with my boot, it tumbles off an empty hole.

The head has been moved.

But why?

I examine the ground for any indication of what has happened. It is too difficult to track people, with the leaves forming a crushed mat on the forest floor. There are a few snapped twigs, and I follow them deeper into the trees, but catch no sight of anyone.

Have the volva returned and done something with the head? And where would the body be? Was it a woman, as Kitta said?

And what has become of Suka?

I find a longer stick on the ground and use it to poke about the leaf-strewn circle. By the time the sun begins its descent, I must admit there is no body to be found. Remembering my promise to meet Atli at dusk, I race toward our sparring field, eager to catch him before the evening meal.

He lies sprawled in the grass, hand on his sword. At the sight of his prone body, untamed thoughts weaken my knees—I have visions of Atli's blond head, bloody and torn from its strong body.

I hold my breath as I near his unmoving side. He snorts and sits up, and I release my breath in a rush.

"I left early to meet you," he begins, worry etched in the youthful lines of his face. "Your husband asked many questions, but I walked away without answering."

"Leave Ref to me." I know the boy does not want to appear weak to the men. I drop to the ground beside him. "I lied to you earlier. We will not train today. Instead, I need you to help me. You patrol in two nights, when the moon is waning, do you not? Who goes with you—an Icelander?"

He shakes his head. "I will be with one of our own, Jokul."

I stretch in the sun, allowing it to soak into my bones. Things are coming together as I had hoped. "That night, I want you to watch the birch grove—the area with the large rock. If you see the volva meeting there, go behind my hut and scratch near the midden heap. I will know it is you and if Ref asks, I will say it's a squirrel."

Atli doesn't question my orders. "Shall I stay away from the volva, m'lady? They are very friendly with me."

I take in his wavy hair and blond beard, his earnest blue eyes, and the muscles straining at his tunic sleeves. The poor boy has no idea how attractive he is to women. "I have noticed. Ignore them, but don't go out of your way to do so. If they are friendly, respond."

I don't want to alert them as I try to discover their intentions for Vinland and Brattahlid. But as surely as I can wield a knife, when I find out what their plans are, I will be the one to thwart them.

ELEVEN

TWO DAYS HAVE PASSED, and I have not been able to find Suka, although Tyr and I have tried to track his path.

Oblivious to our loss, the Icelanders have been busy with their own work, and their longhouse begins to come together swiftly. Until they can build individual huts, they will all sleep in the longhouse on the wall benches.

Valdis and her women spend more time in their own camp, which is farther from the shore than ours. Although I miss the food they prepared for meals, Dagmar and Huld are doing an adequate job of filling my crew's stomachs.

Kitta sleeps in the hut next to us, with my old servant-women. She has told Valdis I might have birthing problems, so she needs to stay nearby. Of course this is a lie, but Valdis believed it—or so it seemed. I know she wishes for Kitta to inform her on my comments and my actions, but Kitta will do no such thing.

The trees have finished changing colors and in just a few days, they will begin to shed their leaves. Yesterday, the white-gray clouds formed a ring around the sun, and the air has lightened and changed scent. Snow will soon arrive, and I wonder if the Icelanders will have a roof over their longhouse before it does.

I poke at my evening meal, wishing again that I had paid attention when Gudrid tried to show me how to cook. The rabbit meat has been scorched through, and the cabbage gives off a putrid smell. Ref sits at my side, watching my every bite. Finally, I turn and glare at him.

"What is wrong with you? You haven't spoken to me in two days. And now you stalk me like a wolf in the brush."

He eats a bite of cabbage and chews it, offering no response to my prodding. Finally, he answers, speaking to the fire instead of to my face.

"It was foolish to send those Icelanders away from our chopping. Now they feel certain we plot against them. Helgi spoke to me today—"

"Helgi? That pithless coward. Why did he not come to me?"

Ref slides an arm around my chair, leaning in toward my ear. "Because he does not trust you, Freydis."

I hate his scolding tone, but I must acknowledge the truth of his words. I begin to stand, but Ref's strong hand grasps my waist and he pulls me back down to my seat. And yet he does not say a word.

My men have seen this, and I feel embarrassed that my husband was able to handle me in such a way. I am the leader of this crew.

"Perhaps I do harbor ill-will against the Icelanders," I hiss. "Suka has been missing for three days. Tyr has tried to track him, but you have not, nor have you allowed my crew to stop their chopping and make a search. What if those Icelanders did him harm? You know they distrust Skraelings of any kind."

Ref turns to me, his voice surprisingly relaxed. "What do I care about that man? We are better off with him gone from our camp."

My body seems to freeze from the inside out, stiffening my spine. Has Ref harmed Suka? He has never spoken to me of Suka's foolish attack on Gudrid at Straumsfjord. Although I can't recall much about the day our men came into the woods to retrieve me from Suka's keeping, I remember very clearly Ref's tenderness with me that night, when I was coming out of my stupor. How he caressed my freshly-cleaned hair, how he held me as I drifted to sleep. He even sang to me, as if I were a small child.

Sometimes my husband's love feels so relentless, I need to tear away from it. His affections are too complete, too splendid. I can never render the same depths of love back toward him. I have no such depths.

Forest children survive best on their own.

A persistent scratching at the wall of my hut edges into my mind, then wakes me with a start. I sit upright in bed, nearly rousing Ref, but he is exhausted from his chopping today and from our time together tonight. Quite often, I find it easier to speak my devotion with my body than my words.

In the dim firelight, I shift through clothing on the pegs until I find Ref's discarded trousers. I step into them and belt them tightly, then pull one of his woolen tunics over my head. Men's clothing is much faster to put on, as well as safer when walking into the underbrush of the forest at night.

I strap on another belt for my sword, tucking the tunic and my cape into it. By the time I pull on my seal-skin boots, I probably look like one of the lumbering black bears of this land.

I slip out the door. Atli waits just outside, eager to give me news. His lantern sits on a nearby tree stump.

"The volva have set up their torches in the grove tonight. I did not linger, but rushed back to tell you. Jokul is walking the shoreline, so we have some time before I must meet up with him again."

I pat his shoulder. Though he has grown since we weighed anchor in Vinland, he has yet to reach my height.

He also does not have my experience creeping around this terrain in the darkness. Both at Straumsfjord and here in Vinland, I have made a practice of visiting the woods at night, feeling my way along the rocks and fallen limbs. This way I know I will be comfortable if we are ever wakened to an unexpected Skraeling attack.

I take up the lantern and lead the way, since the half-moon is covered with clouds. Atli keeps up with me easily, which is encouraging. The boy truly does have the makings of a great Viking warrior.

While we are still out of sight, I put out the flame. Taking Atli's hand, I place it on my belt. If we move together toward the volva circle, I can control the noise of our advance.

Loud as a scream, lights from the grove escape the tight tree limbs as we approach. Most people would have the sense to leave volva alone in their rituals, afraid of seeing something otherworldly. I am too curious to be afraid—or perhaps too angry.

The thrumming beat of a skin drum meets our ears first, followed by a chanting in deep women's tones. The ancient phrases they mutter are not unfamiliar, but hearing them spoken this way almost gives them physical form. The words flow from life to death, from ocean to sky to the earth we stand on. I can imagine the ground coming to life, rising up to fold us into it.

I begin to sway, understanding the blood and the power behind this chant. Atli grips tighter to my belt, bringing me back to myself. I remove his hand and settle on the ground.

"Cover your mouth and nose," I say, covering mine with the bottom of my borrowed tunic. "They are burning the seeds."

The drumming becomes heavier, more frantic. I crawl closer, catching a glimpse of the women. Valdis holds a golden bowl in both hands, eyes closed. Her white hair is wild and unbraided, falling over her bare shoulders. She wears numerous jeweled rings and arm bands.

And nothing else.

All the volva are naked.

I block Atli's view. The women swirl and dance, making weaving movements with their hands. Perhaps all this activity keeps them warm. Or maybe they have partaken of herbs that cause them to be unaffected by the cold.

As Valdis dips her fingertips into the water and sprinkles it over the rock, Atli tugs at my sleeve. I ignore it, certain the volva are preparing for a sacrifice.

When I feel another insistent tug, I turn, ready to scold the vexing Atli. Instead, a hand closes tight around my mouth, even as another folds over my sword hand, clasping it in a fearsome grip.

TWELVE

MY EYES WIDEN BUT I relax into the man's grip, plotting a way to attack. As the torches slant beams of light toward us, I begin to make out the features of the one who holds me captive.

Suka.

"Freydis," he whispers.

I let the reality of his presence sink in, then give a reassuring nod of my head. He slowly unwraps his hands.

"Did you have to do that?" I ask.

"I knew the sight of me would shock you, and you might react without thinking." He scoots closer in the leaves, pushing Atli aside.

Although I can't see the boy's face, I can thank him for his persistent warnings. "Thank you, Atli. It was for the best. Given my entranced state, I might have shouted."

Suka murmurs, "The volva are using henbane seeds; I am sure of it. How else could they remain unaffected by the cold?" His dark, liquid eyes turn back to the light. He sees the volva's state of undress but does not react. He has seen mine, too, when he had to dress me after I lost my child.

I place a hand on Suka's arm. "Where have you been? Tyr is desperate to find you. He has grown tired of our conflicted camp. He is ready to return home to his Skraeling wife."

A growl escapes Suka's lips. "He has no wife now."

"But...what has happened? How do you know this? You have not had time to return to the Skraeling camp."

Suka shakes his head. "I have not done that. I have hidden myself here, in the woods. We both know what a haven the woods can be."

When he pauses, I place my hand on his, encouraging him to continue. Drumbeats rise in the silence of the night, the trills of volva voices arching along with them.

His words come out thick and ragged. "She is dead, Freydis, because the volva murdered her."

My grip tightens, nearly crushing Suka's fingers. But he does not pull back from it, understanding my reaction.

"You are sure?" I breathe out.

"Yes. That night in the longhouse, Valdis threatened me. She said her Icelanders do not tolerate Skraelings, from Greenland or Vinland. She said we had to leave immediately."

I relax my grip. "So you pretended to leave camp, without Tyr?"

"Yes—Tyr is Norwegian, so I knew he would be safe enough. But along the shoreline, I found another skinboat, and I recognized it as the one Tyr had made for his wife. For some reason, she traveled all the way here. Perhaps their village was under attack, or perhaps sickness had struck—I do not know. But she was nowhere to be found."

Atli and I sit motionless, waiting for Suka to finish speaking.

He continues. "I hid the boat and slept in the forest until early morning. Then I searched for Tyr's wife. I found no tracks, nothing. But then I saw you approach the grove. I watched from a distance."

I blush in the darkness, embarrassed to think of Suka watching me sway in the treetop, or the way I vomited when I discovered the head.

He continues, his voice charged with hatred. "When you left, I dug up the grass I saw you move. I recognized the head—what was left of it—as Tyr's wife. She had a dark spot on her forehead that still remained. I took her head so Tyr could give her a proper burial, although I could not find her body."

"Nor could I," I whisper. The chanting has grown quieter, and the torchlight is waning. Perhaps the volva are ready for sleep. I would like to send them to an eternal sleep. I drop my hand to my sword.

"We will kill them all here and now," I say.

Suka lays his hand on mine. "This is not the time. First, we must bring Tyr news of his wife. And you cannot expect to kill the women without going to war with the brothers and their entire crew."

He is right, although I cannot bear it.

"But what of Tyr's wrath? And mine?"

"We will watch for the best time. But not yet. I will stay hidden. Beyond the forest, beyond the hills, I can make camp where smoke from my fire will not be noticed."

Atli shifts. The ground grows cold and uncomfortable, and we need to go before the volva leave for their longhouse.

I pat Suka's leg, thankful he is not dead. "No more talking. We will pretend we know nothing." I grasp Atli's tunic, pulling him toward me. "You understand?"

"Yes, m'lady," he whispers.

"I will not even speak of it to my husband." As I think of Ref, I realize I have been out of our hut for too long. He may wake and notice my absence.

"Now we will scatter," I command. I do not need to say more. The men jump to their feet and Suka offers his hand to pull me up. He is unusually protective of me. Has he guessed I am with child?

Ref still sleeps soundly when I slip into our hut. I try to warm my cold feet by the fire, wondering how those volva managed to stay out in the bracing air for so long, completely undressed.

I try to imagine how they captured Tyr's wife. Did they entice her with a warm drink, filled with herbs to make her sleep? Or did they knock her on the head, leaving her lolling on the ground?

How easily I could have killed them tonight, slitting each pale, unprotected throat like so many wild beasts. And they are animals, that is certain. No higher motive restrains them from killing…and eating…more of our crew.

But Suka was wise in his counsel. I must wait until I have planned a more complete attack, perhaps one that would enable me to take their ship so I can carry more plunder of my own.

Yes, I will wait. But not a moment too long.

As each day passes, I watch the Icelanders. They finally have a sod roof on their longhouse, which is necessary, because snow has started to fall.

Kitta stays close to Dagmar and Huld, helping them prepare food for our men. This has helped me, because I can finally eat my food without gagging or vomiting it back up. Kitta tells me I am still too thin, but I am thankful for my build, which hides the tiny babe's body well. Ref has not yet noticed how my dresses begin to swell under my beltline.

I have taken food to Suka twice at his small camp, even though I know he can survive well enough on his own. Each time, he has warned me not to give in to my hatred.

Today, when I bring him thick strips of salted deer meat, he is clearly distressed.

"I have buried the head of Tyr's wife, but I still cannot uncover her body. We must tell him that I am still alive, but that his wife is dead."

"Shall I bring him to see you here?"

"That would probably be best. Tyr is a giant, and though he is slow to anger, when he loses someone, he becomes unpredictable."

We both remember Tyr's open wailing at Straumsfjord when his Norwegian friend, Sindri, had his head cracked open by a Skraeling. In revenge, I killed the murderous Skraeling that same day.

"I will bring him," I say.

Suka becomes thoughtful, sitting on a rock and pulling his leather boot straps tighter. When he looks up at me, his eyes glisten. "Freydis. I must ask if you are with child again?"

I look to the low-limbed pine tree on my right, nearly overtaken by a sudden urge to climb it and escape this conversation. Should I be honest?

He smiles sadly, not waiting for my answer. "I thought so. Your cheeks are more plump."

I stand, frozen to the ground, as light snowflakes begin to gather on my hair.

"Ref is a fortunate man, to be married to such a warrior as you, and now you will give him a child."

I nod.

He stands, placing both hands on my shoulders. "You are not ill with this babe?"

Again, I nod, unable to speak the words I should say.

He moves his hands down my shoulders, clasping my thin hands in his warm grip. "Do not fear. I will pray that God will protect this child."

I snort. "What god are you praying to?"

"Gudrid's God—the Christ. He hears my prayers now that I have believed."

"That sounds like magic. The volva chant to Odin, and look where he has led them."

Suka's eyes darken. "They have led themselves. Odin is a dead god, Freydis. This Christ is alive. And he will make us alive when we die."

I yank my hands from his, wrapping them around my arms and running them up and down to warm myself. Suka rushes to drape his cloak around me.

"I understand that you do not believe. But we all must believe in something more powerful than ourselves."

I shake my head. "That is not true. I have done well putting all my trust in my own might."

He wraps his arms around me, slowly pulling me into the warmth of his chest. I try not to look at his face, but his voice is filled with concern.

"And yet you must admit that you control nothing. I remember very well what happened in Straumsfjord."

I pull back, knowing he is speaking of how my mind unraveled after my stillbirth. I could not even care for myself, much less admit my son was dead.

Suka continues to push. "When the time comes, who can you ask for help? Friends and family will fail you, as we know. But the Christ does not fail us or leave us alone."

I take another step away from him. "I will thank you not to interfere with my life, Suka. I am happy to be alone."

Yanking his blue cloak from my arms, I throw it back to him before stomping back into the forest.

My own words echo in my ears: *I am happy to be alone.*

Perhaps this is true.

Or perhaps I am the biggest coward of all.

THIRTEEN

WHEN I RETURN TO our longhouse, Kitta is sliding carrots and herbs into the soup pot from the chopping board. Dagmar and Huld are nowhere in sight—probably washing clothing by the creek.

Kitta's plain white overdress emphasizes the darkness of her hair, eyebrows, and lashes. She glances up at me, and I am struck by the natural warmth in her blue eyes. She is the sort of woman who can obtain whatever she wants simply by looking helpless.

She is the sort of woman I could never be.

Stirring the broth, she asks, "Where have you been this fine day? On the hunt? No luck?"

"I have no fresh meat for the mid-day meal, if that is what you are asking."

Her smile wavers. "Oh, no. We have plenty of food. Your serving women have been using our supply sparingly—perhaps a bit too sparingly. Not to speak badly of their efforts."

I can't help but smile. "Efforts" is an apt description of their cooking. "I'll have something to eat before the others return, Kitta. I have work of my own to do today."

She bustles to the back room, returning with a plate of fresh-cooked cod and peas. As she adds flatbread and greens, I nod in appreciation. "You have made this meal especially for me?"

"Yes, I did. Your man brought in fish early this morning and said it was for you, because you enjoy it." I catch the slight flush that creeps up her pale cheeks. "How he does care for you. I have never seen a husband so devoted."

I cut into the flaky fish, weighing Kitta's words. It is true that Ref seeks to please me, but it would be better if he agreed with my decisions instead of questioning them. Probably Finnbogi is a more devoted husband to Valdis—he seems to bend to her every whim.

I lick the salt from my lips. "This fish is tasty. Have you seen Tyr today?"

"The large blond visitor? I believe he is stacking wood with the others nearby."

It does not take me long to finish the delicious food, and I rise and take my leave of Kitta. Dagmar stands outside, teetering on a wooden stool while she hangs the wet clothing on a line. I hope she does not fall and break a foot, or even worse, her back.

"M'lady. We are going inside soon to help serve the mid-day meal."

"Thank you, Dagmar. I am sure Kitta will be grateful."

She clings to the woven line so tightly, I'm afraid it will snap. "Oh, no, m'lady, Kitta will be returning to the Icelanders' longhouse to serve their meal. Part of her duty, she said."

The old woman turns back to her task, and I mull over her words. So Kitta is not staying away from Valdis, as I instructed her to do.

Has she told Valdis I know of her murder of the Skraeling woman?

If so, what would that volva witch do to keep me silent? I am certain her husband is unaware of what she does in her pagan ceremonies.

I stride down the path, lost in thought. As I try to picture what a total war with Valdis would look like, I stumble onto our crew, working closer to the camp than I thought. Tyr is nowhere to be found. Ref stacks wood, his back toward me. I sidle up to Thorgrim. "Where is Tyr?"

He shakes his head. "You won't like this, m'lady, but he's over with the other crew. They needed a tall man to help daub the upper chinking."

Of course they did. They are doing all these things behind my back, because they know Ref will not stand up to them.

I nod shortly and edge back into the trees, moving toward the Icelanders' campsite. When I catch sight of the clearing, I am surprised to see how they have built their longhouse into the very ground. It has a low roof, and does not stretch very far to house so many. This must be an Icelandic building method.

Sure enough, Tyr's tall blond head stretches above the rest. He dips into a pail, then smears mud between the top logs of the wall. The lower wall is already covered in turf.

Valdis emerges to say something to Tyr, and he responds with a rolling laugh. If the man knew what she had done to his wife, he would tear her very head off.

I do not know how Suka can soften the blow when he informs Tyr of the truth. And why should Tyr have to wait for revenge? Why should I wait to protect my camp from the poisonous evil of a woman who eats flesh and forces her followers to eat it?

Helgi and another man grip side ropes on a riveted bench, carrying it into the longhouse. It is plain to see there is no board built into the bottom of it, and I am reminded of our benches at Brattahlid. My father had tunnels dug underneath select benches to provide escape routes into nearby fields.

He used to say, "They'll not catch me with my trousers off, even if they are," then roar with laughter. Thankfully, none of my father's enemies dared make shore in Greenland, where most of the residents were loyal to him, grateful he had discovered a new land for them to settle.

Still, it is true that both my father and I have no trouble making enemies.

It will probably be easy to discover what my enemies plot in the privacy of their own longhouse. I will search for an outlying tunnel that will lead me underneath that bench.

Soft but steady footsteps sound behind me. I tumble into the soft, leafy earth behind a mushroom-covered fallen log.

Kitta strides past, eyes fixed on the new longhouse. As she approaches, two of Valdis' women rush out to meet her, tittering and pointing at Tyr behind his back. The forward blonde who flirted with Atli now seems to have shifted her attentions to our Norse visitor.

What if Valdis killed Tyr's wife so he would not feel tied to the Skraelings she hopes to overthrow? What if she is luring him into her camp? She knows he is a fearsome warrior.

She is surprisingly confident to assume he will not discover what she has done.

I will make sure he hears the gut-wrenching truth today.

FOURTEEN

I HIDE IN THE forest between camps until Tyr returns. When he finally does, the sun is high and he chews energetically on a piece of flatbread wrapped tight around meat. Of course those volva fed him. They know how to impress men.

When I drop from my low tree limb, he jumps, releasing his food to grip his knife hilt. I feel less than sorry for making him waste his meal.

He relaxes his grip when he recognizes me. "Freydis! Why are you hiding like that?"

"Perhaps I should ask what you are doing over *there* with those Icelanders."

He shrugs. "They needed a tall man to fill the chinks in their longhouse."

I stare at him.

He stumbles for words to fill the silence. "They promised me a hearty meal."

My stare does not lessen. He finally gives up.

"What do you want with me, Freydis? I have done nothing

wrong. I will soon leave your camp and return to my wife and her people. I have caused you no trouble."

I snatch his large hand, pulling him along for a few steps. "There is something you must know. Come with me."

Reluctantly, the large warrior trails behind me. We exchange no more words until we pass the final hill, where we can see smoke from Suka's fire.

"What is the meaning of this?"

I turn, looking up at the man's powerful jaw and pale eyes. I wish we could keep him in our camp as one of our own warriors, but when he hears of his wife's murder, there is no telling what he will do.

"Suka is alive." I gesture toward his small camp.

His eyes widen, but he recovers quickly. He begins to run toward the fire. Too late, I realize the black smoke hangs too heavy in the air. Why has Suka let his fire smolder? He must know the smoke plumes will be visible above these hills—perhaps by the Icelanders.

Even as we draw closer, Suka does not emerge. I shout for his attention. When there is no reply, we scour the area, looking for hints as to his whereabouts. Perhaps he grew tired of hiding and decided to return to our camp?

I suggest this to Tyr, but his eyes reflect the same worry as mine. When we finally turn to go back to camp, Tyr grabs my shoulders and blocks my path. I try not to react to the wildness of his grip.

"There is something you hide from me. I know Suka well, and he would not turn tail and run unless he feared for his life. Or maybe he wanted to protect someone. Why did he abandon camp without telling me?"

Lying seems to be the best choice in this situation, at least until Suka returns and can inform Tyr of his wife's death.

I nearly stumble over a heap lying on the ground. Bending over the dirty fabric, I pick it up. It is Suka's blue cloak. He would never discard such a fine-woven cloak so carelessly.

I do not know how they did it, for I watched them rambling in and out of their longhouse all morning. But something deep in my gut tells me the volva have taken Suka.

Tyr examines the cloak and confirms that it belongs to Suka. His eyes darken, but he does not speak, respecting my silence.

I wrestle with the best course of action. Should I tell Tyr and risk being in harm's way if he loses control? Or should I wait until we are back at camp, where Atli and my men could protect me?

I meet his eyes, knowing what I would want if one of my loved ones had been murdered. And I know what Suka would want me to do.

"Sit on the ground," I command. I will speak from a position of strength.

Tyr hesitates, but obeys, awkwardly tumbling into a sitting position. He stretches his long legs out and peers up at me.

Knowing I could crush him in any number of ways when he is in this disabled position, I begin to explain. I cannot soften my words, as Gudrid does, so it does not take long for me to come around to the disgusting pith of the story: the volva killed and then ate part of his Skraeling wife.

And now they have most likely taken his best friend.

Tyr takes deep, gasping breaths as if he is preparing to dive underwater. I step closer, standing next to his lower legs, but just out of reach. I only thought to bring my curved knife today, but I am sure I could slice him with it or stab him before he could hurt me, should the need arise.

He leans forward, his voice thick with emotion. "By the gods, I loved her. I never thought I could love a Skraeling, after they killed Sindri. In truth, Suka and I had planned an attack on my wife's village. But she surprised us where we hid in the undergrowth, and she smiled." He begins to weep, mindlessly repeating himself. "She smiled."

His anguished eyes search for mine. "She will never smile again. She will not bear me children. I forgave the Skraelings; I accepted them."

I nod, maintaining my watchful stance.

He continues. "But that witch will never accept them, Freydis. She is not like the other volva, although it is true they perform human sacrifices. She is unnatural, to eat the…the flesh of a human. I have heard her women mention her hatred for the natives here, but I never thought it would push her so far."

He shifts as if he is ready to stand, but I place my foot on his leg. "Not yet."

Grasping my hesitance, he relaxes into a sitting position. "Now we must find Suka and tell the others at camp."

"No. We can tell no one yet. Suka said we must wait until we are strong enough to fight their entire crew. This will require scouting and stealth."

"I will wait for your word," he says.

"I know you will, because you want this attack to be successful as much as I do. And as for Suka...I will watch the birch grove tonight, to be sure they do not try to murder him as they did your wife."

"I will come with you."

The weight of our task falls on me like an avalanche. What if they plan to sacrifice Suka this very night? Yes, Tyr and I together could surely kill every one of the volva. But could we alert our men in time, prepare the camp for war when the Icelanders learn of their women's fate?

I know what Gudrid would do. First, she would pray to her Christ. Then, she would tell her husband everything. But Thorfinn Karlsefni is a very different man than my Ref—Thorfinn is a leader. Would Ref believe me, or would the cannibalism of the volva even alarm him? He has no fondness for Suka.

It is true he would not want me taking these risks, especially if he knew I am with child. But would he see the need to battle the Icelanders? He is dubious enough when I tell him the volva hate me. Perhaps he will think I have contrived this story to take over the Icelanders' ship, which he knows I want.

No, Ref cannot know of our plans. He can continue to flout my judgment, sending members of our crew to aid the Icelanders. They will be less suspicious if Ref remains friendly.

I cannot be friendly to a flesh-eating murderer. Instead, I will busy myself with laying a trap Valdis can't slide out of, snake that she is.

FIFTEEN

OF COURSE, ON THE one night I need to watch for Suka, Ref has the sudden impulse to talk with me.

I know Tyr waits outside the grove, probably freezing in this weather. It has suddenly turned icy and the snow is falling fast. I have checked back on Suka's campsite twice, and I've had Atli check it as well. He has not returned.

A chill runs through me once again. Suka could be lying on the hard ground, dazed and senseless, unable to protect himself from those chanting, dancing killers.

And yet Ref sits on our bed, motioning me over to sit with him. He has been speaking all evening about the craftsmanship of the Icelanders' longhouse. Does he not realize how I hate that wretched crew?

He continues, either oblivious to my irritation or choosing to ignore it—I really can't tell which. "Valdis offered us fermented shark meat from Iceland. She said they brought extra for our crew, and it would be a shame if we did not try some."

"Shame or not, we will not eat their shark, Ref. We won't have her food in our camp, ever."

His eyes meet mine. My gaze drifts from one eye to the other, never tiring of their contrast—one is green as jade, with a thin thread of sunny yellow circling it, and one is fjord blue. If they had been the same color, they would not have held me in such thrall. Those eyes may well be the only power Ref has over me.

He blinks, then turns to stare at the fire. "Then that is that. I will tell her we will not accept the meat. Though I admit I do love shark."

I want to smack his face. He may as well say he prefers her food over mine.

But he is lost in thought, speaking whatever comes to mind. "Also, Valdis asked if Kitta is doing well in our camp. I did not know the girl was staying over here."

Thankfully, an easy explanation presents itself, and I blurt it out. "I needed a new cook. Dagmar and Huld ruin the meat I work hard to provide."

He sighs. "You are not the only provider around here—you know I go fishing nearly every other day. Did you not enjoy the cod I brought for you?"

I wave his words away like fluttering moths. He has no idea what I do for this camp. As wind whistles around our hut, I am reminded of my duty tonight.

I take my wool cape from a peg. "I do not have time for talking, Ref. I told Atli I would help him guard the camp tonight." As he stands to protest, I shake my head. "Do not think about taking my place. I *do* know what you do for the camp, and that your muscles must be sore from days and days of chopping, to say nothing of how early you must rise to fish. You should drink your mead and sleep sound tonight."

Again, he tries to object. "It is bitter cold tonight, and getting colder. You are so thin, my wife, I fear you might freeze through."

I smile, pulling on woolen socks and boots before rising to strap on my sword. "I am still younger than you, old man. Warm your bones while I serve my crew. But take comfort—I will not guard again while we are here."

As I begin to lift the latch, a knock sounds on the door. Surely Tyr would not have tried to meet me here, in front of my husband?

But Kitta stands outside, her pale face peeking from the soft velvet folds of her cape. "I came to check on you," she says.

Ref cannot know of my condition, the true reason Kitta stays nearby. But it is too late. He strides up behind me, laying a hand on my shoulder.

"Kitta? Is something wrong?"

I give a barely-noticeable shake of my head, and Kitta's sharp eyes catch it. "I was checking to see if Freydis needed any food. I know she was out much of the day and only pecked at her evening meal." Surprising me further, she pulls out a waxed cloth, opening it to reveal cheese and…

"Is that fermented shark?" I ask sharply.

She nods, confused. "The others had extra and offered it to me."

I raise my chin, giving a careless toss of my hair. "I won't be having that. You are free to feed it to Ref, though. The man simply loves shark. He cannot get enough of it."

I stalk into the night without looking back.

In the forest, I nearly trip over Tyr. He lies on the ground in a heap, cloak drawn over his head. I drop to his side in the darkness. "Have you seen them?"

"No. Not one movement in the grove."

Perhaps it is too cold for the volva to work their naked magic tonight. Perhaps they never took Suka at all.

Or perhaps he is dead already.

Time seems to crawl. I shove my quickly-numbing hands in my cape, then begin blowing on them. My breath mixes with the snowflakes, adding to their frozen stiffness. Tyr must notice my feeble efforts, because he wordlessly hands me his wool gloves. I was a fool to walk out without them.

An owl blasts its tooting call above our heads. Light, careful steps sound deeper in the forest, but they belong to an animal, not a human.

My feet finally give in to the icy wetness, cramping up in pain. I know the big man at my side must be even colder than I.

"We must return to camp, Tyr. The women are not out tonight. Who is guarding?"

"Atli, and I was supposed to join him."

"Go and find him, then, since it is doubtless time to switch the guard. That way you can go inside to your fire." It is convenient Atli is out tonight, in case Ref feels the need to check my story.

"I will call him." To my surprise, Tyr raises his hands to his mouth and gives a convincing stag's call. There is no reply. He repeats his call, staggering around on his numb feet as he does so, but there is still no answer.

"He should be able to hear you?" I ask.

"Surely. I told him not to wander too far from this area."

Rising desperation creeps into Tyr's voice, a desperation I have started to feel myself. Atli would never abandon his post—unless someone dragged him from it.

SIXTEEN

SINCE WE ARE TEETERING on the edge of frostbite, we must return to our huts, even though we are unsure where Atli has disappeared to. Tyr has been out too long, and he leans heavily on me as we trudge through the snow back to camp. I have seen one of my father's men treat frostbite during an abnormally cold winter, and I instruct Tyr to take the same steps—use the hot water from his kettle, mix it with cold water, then ease his feet into it. Then he must dry and wrap them and stay in bed. I offer to help, but he refuses.

"If your Ref discovered you came into my hut, I don't know what would happen."

I laugh. "Ref will do nothing but what I tell him to do."

I can't see Tyr's eyes, but I can feel them on my face. "You think so little of your husband's jealousy?"

I fall silent, allowing myself to enter the deeper places of my heart for just a moment. I have assumed Ref has no jealousy for me, because he let Suka carry me off to the caves after I lost our child. Days passed, and my husband never came to retrieve me. I know I was out of my mind with grief, but it seems if Ref had any real love for me, he would not have let another man care for me in my weakened state.

A surety passes over me, swift and sickening. My husband cannot bear to see me weak, because I am his strength.

I take my leave of Tyr, listening for any movement in the camp that could be Atli, but there is none. I long to search for him, but I could lose my toes or even endanger my child in this cold.

As I slip into our door, Ref shifts on the bed. I creep closer and touch his arm. He is sprawled onto my side of the bed, but he is deep in sleep.

Silently, I warm myself by the fire, hoping Tyr is taking the measures I suggested. The last thing we need is for such a warrior to lose a toe or finger.

Under the warm blankets, sleep begins to darken my senses, until a vision of Suka's severed head floats on the ceiling above me. A sudden chill racks my body. His eyes are frozen open, fully darkened. His lips are twisted in an unfamiliar scowl.

I press the length of my body alongside Ref's, hoping to quell my violent shivering. He gives a contented, half-wakened groan in response, rolling toward me and draping an arm over me.

It is only right that he know about this babe, regardless of who has fathered it. I will tell him tomorrow.

Sunlit snowflakes drift in through the smoke hole, tickling me awake. Ref has already left my side, probably to go fishing.

A thud sounds on my door, like someone throwing a stuffed sack of barley against it. As I stand, my clothing feels unusually heavy. I look down only to realize I went to sleep fully dressed in my shift, overdress, and woolen socks. I strap on my belt with my knife, then pad over to the door.

When I crack it, something slumps into the room. A lifeless body.

Atli.

A slow scream begins to make its way up my throat, pushing its way out like a roar.

Blond, unkempt hair spills over my arm as I struggle to pull the boy up. Placing my fingers on his dirty throat, I'm relieved to find a flickering throb of blood beneath his skin. He lives.

Dagmar rushes to my side, her eyes bleary with sleep. Obviously the old woman was not up with the sun this morn. Perhaps she is becoming more lazy now that Kitta is in our camp.

"I heard you, m'lady. What is wrong with the boy? Shall I fetch something to drink?"

"Yes. And rouse Tyr and tell him to come to me at once."

"Yes, m'lady." She blinks rapidly as if trying to increase alertness, then stumbles away.

I look over Atli's fingers, fearing he was frostbitten last night. But they are warm, although somewhat pale. His eyes remain closed despite my handling, almost as if he has fainted.

What has that witch done to him?

Tyr's boots thud up the path, and he squats to examine the boy. He silently meets my gaze, questioning.

I make a guess. "Perhaps it is the henbane seeds, or some type of poison. We will take him into my hut so Kitta can work with him—she knows of the herbs Valdis uses. It is better if we look for Suka."

Tyr nods. He bends to pick the boy up, tossing him easily over his shoulder. He carefully positions Atli's limp body on my bed. Dagmar returns, carrying a drinking horn and wet cloths. Huld trails along after her, wearing only her shift. I should not have forced these old women to make this journey. They will be just as useless caring for Atli as they are at cooking.

"I need Kitta in here. Wake her. You two will prepare the midday meal."

Huld yawns, trying to stretch her crooked back. "Yes, m'lady."

Dagmar looks surprised, but nods her white head. I cringe, thinking of the tasteless meal we will have to stomach today.

When the room is empty, Tyr and I discuss where we will search for Suka. We know the volva did not take him to the grove last night, so Tyr will examine the farther-flung areas and I will comb the forests.

A short knock sounds and I open the door. Kitta steps inside. Her hair is hastily knotted and the back of her cloak is caught in her belt. Her eyes rove the hut until she spots Atli's body. Rushing to the bedside, she reaches into a leather pouch on her belt, pulling out carved rune stones, which she begins to position on his chest.

I interrupt this useless practice, anxious for real healing. "What have they done to him?"

Using her fingertip, she gently raises his eyelids, which only provokes a slight shift of his head. "I do not know. She has put a forgetting spell upon him, perhaps."

I clench my fists. "This is no spell. This is a poison of some sort." If only Gudrid were here, she would discern what herbs were used. Kitta is blinded by her long-ingrained fear of the volva's magic.

Kitta looks thoughtful. "I suppose it could be the henbane or one of her other herbs. There is nothing for it but to watch him closely. I will sponge water over his face in hopes he will wake."

I know a better way—one Kitta can actually help me with. I smile. "You have gone inside the new longhouse, haven't you?"

She hesitates, then gives a slow, guilty nod. "I had to feed their crew as they finished the building. I knew you would not want me to, but Valdis insisted."

I hate those words: *but Valdis*. I want this girl to respect me—to fear me. I want her first hesitation to be *but Freydis*.

Shoving these thoughts aside, I fix her with an unblinking stare. "I believe she has an escape bench, doesn't she, with a tunnel beneath it?"

Kitta nods quickly. "I heard Helgi speak of it, yes."

I step closer, nearly toe to toe with her boots. "And where did he say it comes out?"

She does not waver, her blue eyes wide. "By three flat rocks on their side of the creek."

I have heard enough. I turn to Tyr, who stands attentive. "Go on. We will meet at the mid-day meal." He nods and strides out, nearly hitting his head on the doorframe.

My limbs are achy and stiff from last night's venture, but I ignore the pain, pulling on my boots and cape for another outdoor trip. This time, I remember to take my woolen gloves.

I leave my sword behind, carrying only my curved knife. The

Icelanders' secret tunnel will be narrow and dark, given the limited time they've had to dig it. Once I'm in, I'll have to trust they have dug it all the way under the longhouse.

Kitta returns to her runestones, chanting. Atli's right leg jerks repeatedly, as if he is trying to kick something off, but no blanket covers him. I hope this is a good sign, but I have no time to dawdle.

In the bracing outdoor air, I pull my cape tighter. Light snowflakes dust my cheeks, offering their bold, tiny kisses. Although the snow has melted a bit in the sunlight, Tyr and I cannot stay out in this bitter weather too long.

I don't want to know how Valdis got close enough to hurt Atli. Maybe she had one of her volva women approach him with some story of distress. Maybe she told him I was in danger.

She will not get close to him again, because I am like the hidden bear lying in tall grass—closer to her than she imagines. She will not see me until it's too late.

SEVENTEEN

KNOWING THE WOODS AS I do, it is not difficult to find the three flat stones. The tunnel opening appears narrow, but not too narrow for me. Probably they intend to widen it in the future.

Crawling in headfirst, my fingers sink into the loose, pebbly dirt. I brace myself for a descent, but the hastily-dug tunnel is not as deep as the ones we had at Brattahlid. Worms flatten beneath my hands and a cold, damp smell fills the air. I am not repulsed by these things—in fact, I feel wrapped in warmth. I am climbing right into the belly of the earth, and the earth has always shown me love.

As my knees and hands begin to tire, a narrow sliver of sunlight pierces the darkness. The ground tilts upward. I will soon be under the bench, inside their longhouse.

Pebbles loosen in a sudden torrent, spilling onto the tunnel floor in front of me. When the deluge is finished, I take a dusty breath, trying not to cough.

As is my habit, I have charged into what could be a deadly situation without a second thought. This tunnel could very well collapse on my head and bury me alive. Or it could collapse behind me, forcing me to escape through the longhouse.

I could kill my child with my recklessness.

Shoving these thoughts aside, I hold to my determination and push forward, crawling over the pile of debris. I have come this far and I will not turn back. If there is a chance I can discover what Valdis did to Atli or to Suka, this risk will be worth it. At this time of day, only the women should be in the longhouse, preparing the mid-day meal.

As I climb up, closer to the splinters of light, the space widens. Stretching out my fingers, I bump into wood. I am in the bench.

I situate myself on the dirt floor, pulling my gloves back on to ward off the chilly dampness. Voices are muffled above me, so I feel for something small to hold the bench lid open. Finding nothing but round pebbles, I finally slip off one of my flat silver brooches and slide it into the crack. Immediately, the voices become clearer.

"So what is our next step?" It is a man's voice, gruff and abrupt. I believe it's Helgi. "Won't she want to retaliate for the boy?"

Valdis laughs. "He's not dead. Just…afflicted by drinking the warm cider Birsa gave him. Never trust a volva bearing gifts."

"It wasn't a light load, carrying him to her doorstep," Hegli complains. "You must have put some special herbs in that brew, because he didn't even stir."

"Nothing different than what I've given the others."

The others? More than one.

Her skirts swish closer as they walk toward the central fire. "I wish I could have seen the look on that bony forest child's face when she found her favored warrior, rendered useless. She must have thought he was dead."

This woman is pure evil.

She continues. "In truth, she is so thin, I doubt she'll be able to carry her babe the full time. I heard she lost her firstborn."

Rage burns inside me. My face is aflame.

Helgi speaks up. "You have plans for the babe?"

"Of course I do. This land must be fully consecrated if we are to successfully occupy it. Others have tried to settle here and they have lost to the Skraelings. Now we have spilled the blood of two Skraelings and taken their power from them. All that remains is the blood of a babe, slain on the sacred stone."

Helgi's voice drops. "And what if Finnbogi hears of your plan to take Freydis' babe?"

Valdis' words lilt with confidence. "My husband will not try to stop me. He fears the gods, and even more, the goddesses who guide me. He knows we are weaving our fate in this land. Besides, he enjoys the company of my young women too much."

Helgi murmurs something, and soon there is nothing to hear but kissing. So they are lovers.

Finally, he speaks again. "When we have settled this land, someone must return to tell Leif of his sister's death."

"Of course. Finnbogi will take my women and return the Greenlandic crew to Leif. Those slaves are rightfully his, and he will be thankful. I doubt Leif will mourn the loss of his sister, since she ran off without telling him in the first place. Then, when the time is right, Finnbogi will send for our allies in Greenland and they will overthrow Leif's farm, so we can use it as a port for our plunder."

"But how will we get to Freydis Eiriksdottir? She is well-protected by her men, and you can see she is bold as the goddess

Freyja herself. Surely her husband will object?"

Valdis huffs. "Doubtless, Freydis is bold, but she is insensitive to men and has little awareness of her female powers of persuasion. Besides, I have been told that she only married Ref for his money. There was hardly a word spoken between them in the longhouse. It is a wonder they live in the same hut. Ref will be easy enough to turn—and I have already begun that process."

Sickness coils in my stomach, like poison from that viper-woman. Every word she has spoken is heartless. She thinks only of herself and her power. I cannot make sense of everything she has said, but I will.

Helgi and Valdis fall silent as the other volva enter the longhouse, singing and laughing. The group trickles toward the rear of the building to prepare the meal.

My breath comes shallow and fast. I cannot allow myself to think through what has been revealed. Even as I reach for my brooch, the bench slams shut with someone's weight. The teetering, triangular silver pin pops out, clinking to the dirt floor outside.

I hold my breath, but soon a woman speaks up. "Whose brooch is this? This doesn't look like one of our blacksmith's designs."

I cannot linger. Carefully twisting around so I can enter the tunnel headfirst, I plunge back into the hole.

By the time I hear the bench creak open, I am halfway back to the creek.

And by the time I reach the door of my hut, I know what I have to do.

EIGHTEEN

ALTHOUGH TYR SITS BY my side at the mid-day meal, Ref positions himself on my other side, so I cannot openly question Tyr about his search.

I fear the worst, given Valdis' claim to have rid the world of two Skraelings. I know she hated Suka, but the question is, how did she discover where he was hiding?

Kitta leans over me to spoon more fish soup into my bowl, and I eagerly slurp at it, trying to fill my empty stomach. Someone's gaze seems to burn into me and I look up. Ref's eyes are fixed on my every bite. No wonder the soup tastes so fresh—he has caught the fish for it.

He waits for my words of appreciation.

Perhaps Tyr was right. Would Ref be jealous of me, jealous enough to do something violent? Valdis said I didn't know how to use my womanly powers. This is true enough. I spend my time telling men what to do, not wooing them to me. I am very nearly one of them.

What if I turned the tables and gave my husband what he wants?

It has always been easier to withhold it so I can maintain my power over him.

"Thank you," I murmur, looking straight ahead. I can't bear to see the open longing in his eyes.

Ref's warm, rough hand cups my own, stilling my spoon on the table. "You are hungrier lately," he says.

Something deep inside twinges, nudging me. This is the time.

I force myself to look at him and hate the way my heart leaps in response to his soft eyes. My husband is devoted to me, with a love I have not earned, a love I can never return.

"I am with child."

His grip tightens and a smile spreads across his rugged face. His eyes glisten with joyful tears. "I wondered. Are you sick at all?"

"I was at the start. I am growing larger now, and my food stays down."

"Your color is good," he says, stroking my cheek.

Tyr watches us in silence. Perhaps he did not know. When I glare at him for staring, he tears off a hunk of bread, chewing on it like a horse with that powerful jaw.

"This is why Kitta has come," Ref continues.

"Yes."

I pull my hand away to finish my soup, unwilling to discuss this further.

As Kitta returns to bring us cooked beets, she seems to notice Ref's lingering smile. As she hands him his bowl, she touches his back. I suppose she is happy for him—most of the camp knows how much he longs to be a father.

But I recall what Valdis said, that she has already begun to turn him. Is Kitta part of this?

"How is Atli?" My words are abrupt, and Kitta jerks her head toward me, hand falling to her side.

"He recovers. I believe he ate or drank potent herbs. He is very thirsty. Huld stays at his side now so I can serve the meal." Her words are not hesitant. She does not need my approval of her actions, unlike my slave wenches.

Perhaps I have no control over this girl at all. But she has to choose.

I shove my curls out of my face, shooting her a look. "I do not want you talking to Valdis or her women again. Nor to any of Finnbogi's men."

The girl tugs the shiny tips of her long hair, a gesture that captures the attention of several of my men. Surely she will not challenge my command?

"Yes, m'lady."

It is the first time she has used this term for me, a term of deference and submission.

It is appropriate.

I eat the beets quickly, to show I am thankful for her cooking, even though they are not my favorite. As I prepare to leave, Ref touches the corner of my lip with his thumb, slowly rubbing it over both lips. "Beet juice," he says simply. He eyes my stained lips in such a way it is obvious what he wants.

I will give it to him and see what happens.

Deliberately, I lean his way, taking his lips in my own like a hungry animal. He is not embarrassed—instead, he deepens our kiss.

Yes, perhaps it is time I started using my power over my husband to my advantage.

After the meal, Ref leads my men back into the woods. But Tyr stays behind, pulling me aside on the path.

His voice is low, although no one stands nearby. "I have not found Suka. What about you?"

I want to shake my head and pretend he is safe. I want to imagine Suka will live out his days in this land, with the freedom he so craved. Instead, I force myself to speak my fears. "I overheard Valdis bragging how she has killed two Skraelings. She might be speaking of him."

Tyr slowly blinks his silver-blue eyes, pressing his fists together until they whiten. He reminds me of Gudrid's bull, the one she released at Straumsfjord when the Skraelings attacked. That bull would kill anything in its path. I hope Tyr is more loyal than an unthinking animal, so he can stand with us in this war with the Icelanders.

Because we are now at war. Attacks have been made, ruthless attacks with no thought for the consequences.

I lay a hand on Tyr's arm. I know I cannot calm him, but I can direct his rage, because I fully share it.

"You will have vengeance for your wife, Tyr. Blood for blood. But I need you to stay strong and under control until I give the command. Then I will need you and all my men to rally alongside me. Can you do this, as Suka wanted?"

Tyr's jaw is tight, but he gives a sharp jerk of his head. He is with me.

Even as I wish I could put this nightmare behind me, Atli struggles out the door of my hut, leaving it wide open behind him.

He is half-dressed and his eyes have a fevered glaze.

He recognizes me and stumbles my way. Tyr catches him as his knees buckle. It is disturbing to see such a healthy, sound young warrior in this state. I go to his side, taking his warm hand in mine.

"You are not well. Tyr will carry you to his hut where he can watch you. I must go and look for Suka—we did not find him last night."

Atli focuses on my eyes, and I am thankful for the color in his face, even if it is patchy. He tries to tell me something, his words croaky and weak.

"The volva poisoned me with the cider. I could not move and they bound me and made me watch." His eyes shift to Tyr's massive arms, which still prop him up. He gulps and wipes a hand across his forehead, sweaty even as he sits in the snow. "It was over that craggy hill beyond our field, m'lady. They cut his throat. Suka. I saw him die. But then—"

He pales as a gag burbles its way up his throat. He retches repeatedly into the snow at his side, vomiting any liquid he may have taken from Kitta.

I hold his forehead, unsure what else to do. In a brief lull, he hastily finishes his thought.

"They *cooked* him, m'lady. To eat. I can't believe—" The vomiting starts up again.

Rage nearly blinds me. "Kitta!" I scream.

Tyr's tense arm muscles match his unblinking stare. Valdis has taken everything from him. As a warrior—as a *human*—he must have revenge.

And so will I.

I am thankful that Kitta does not delay. She quickly takes my place by Atli's side. I know she and Tyr will get him inside where he can continue to recover.

As for me, I will go and find whatever is left of Suka and bury it with a marker. It is the very least I can do for this man who has been such a friend to me—someone who always shielded me from harm.

My child may be his. When it is born, I will know by its eye shape and color. And no matter who its father is, my baby will never be taken from me by the grasping, blood-covered hands of Valdis.

NINETEEN

I TAKE UP MY bow and quiver so I can shoot any volva I see, but I expect they are all asleep after another exhausting night of human sacrifice.

Valdis has overstepped, even for a volva. She must truly believe that eating the flesh of the Skraelings will defeat them as a group. I am amazed she was able to convince anyone to believe her depraved notions.

But some people are gifted with persuasion—wasn't my own father? Eirik the Red convinced many of his friends to leave Iceland and start a new life in Greenland. And I believe I, too, have this gift. Not only did I persuade Ref to come along on this journey, but many of Leif's slaves left the security of the farm to sail with me.

I will have to persuade them again, and soon. I will have to bend them to my will.

My snowy boots begin to seep with water as I trudge through our field. Will Atli be able to train with me again? Will he even be well enough to fight the Icelanders, when the time comes?

Kicking rocks loose as I climb, I finally top the craggy hill, unprepared for what I see in the valley below.

Blood has spattered the snow—great amounts of it. They did not even bother to try to hide it this time, becoming bolder with each killing. Valdis must have been laughing, knowing I watched for her in the birch grove while she was murdering Suka here.

Suka's camp was not obvious. How did she find it and overpower him?

Snow-slicked rocks cover the hill. I will have to sit and slide down, and I cannot do that with my bow and quiver. Locating a thick tree, I prop my weapon behind it.

Shoving my hand into a crack in a boulder, I slowly lower myself between rocks and begin my descent. Valdis chose this place because she knew it would be perilous for me to climb down while I am with child. She has underestimated me again.

I lose my footing several times and slide into rocks, but my feet finally touch flat ground. Heaving my weary body up, I move toward the blood, trying to steel myself for whatever I find. I have seen many hacked limbs in my life, so my stomach is strong toward these things. But my heart is still weak.

Near a clump of low-lying bushes, Suka's boot catches my eye, a thin layer of snow resting on it. His trousers protrude slightly, and I follow their line to find the rest of his body, lying flat on his back as if they murdered him on the ground. Unreasonably, I think how cold he must feel, lying on the snow with no cloak, but I feel thankful the rest of his clothing remains.

I try to hold my eyes back from looking at his tunic to search for his head. But I already know. It is not there. When Atli said they cooked him, he must have meant Suka's head.

I cannot do it. I cannot go closer.

There is so much blood, marring the clean whiteness of the snow. The blood of the bright-eyed man who spoke to me so earnestly of his faith, his heaven.

I hope he is there now. But there will be no redemption for me. I will become the most unmerciful of murderers.

I accept my fate.

At the evening meal, I thread my way through the long tables, stopping to talk to my crew. I call them each by name: Valgerd, Halli, Bork, and so many others. They have sacrificed much to follow me here, and I hope we can gather enough plunder to warrant their courage.

Tyr broods in the carved chair, ignoring his food. He buried what was left of Suka for me, since I could not bring myself to do it. My men instinctively give him extra space tonight.

I tap his wide shoulder. "Eat. You will need your strength tomorrow. Be ready."

At these words, Tyr looks at me, his sadness sliding away and his eyes taking on a shine that reflects an inner fury I share.

Ref watches me move among the men, but when I return to my seat, he doesn't ask questions. Instead, he begins to make small circles on my lower back with the palm of his hand, probably because he noticed I have been pressing my hand to that spot. He thinks the babe is giving me pain, but it is a bruise from the rocks and each time he touches it, I want to yelp.

I knock his hand away. At his shocked look, I hastily gather his hand into my own and hold it tightly. Although I am merely hiding something I don't want to explain, it is comforting to feel each of his fingers tighten around my own. Ref's fingers are neither too thick nor too narrow, the perfect size for intricate work like wood-carving, yet equally adept at manning the sail ropes or swinging a sword.

We sit entwined like this so long I begin to wonder if he can discern my black thoughts. And it is of the highest importance that he does not.

Smooth as a dolphin cutting the water, Kitta moves behind me, carrying a platter with sliced meat. She hesitates, but I motion her forward to question her.

"How is Atli faring? I looked in on him but he was asleep. Has he moved around much?"

Relief floods her face. What did she think I was going to ask? She places several thin pieces of meat on my plate as she answers. "I believe he recovers, but he does babble on and on." She shifts her glance to Ref, then back to me. Her arched eyebrow tells me that she knows of Suka's murder, but is hiding it from my husband with her vague answer.

She is a clever girl. *Too* clever?

I force a smile. "Very good news."

Kitta eases past me and attempts to shift a piece of the slippery meat onto Ref's plate, but it drops to the table instead. She laughs as she retrieves it for him, and I count five men who turn, eyes lapping up her youthful beauty.

My husband is one of those men.

Deep in the night, as Ref breathes soundly, I prepare for what is coming. I force myself to remember the hacked-up head of Tyr's wife. I feel the fear that gripped me when I saw Atli, slumped on my doorstep. I make myself envision Suka's bloody body, lying lifeless on the snow.

I slip from the bed and pull my blue linen overdress over my shift, pinning my favorite silver serpent brooches on either side. Twisting my hair into a simple knot, I use a wide silver comb to secure it.

I sift through my jewel box in the dim light of the fire, until I feel the familiar grooves of my carved wooden pendant. It was a gift from Ref when we married. No one in my family could believe the craftsmanship he had shown, carving runes and sea creatures into the light wood.

I unlatch it, sliding the wooden facing to the side. An interior chamber holds what I seek.

I did not want to do this again, but I have no choice. A glance through the smoke hole in our roof tells me the sun will soon be rising. I dip out a cup of hot water from the pot over the fire, then mix in the bits of mushroom I dried before I left Brattahlid.

Forgive me, I beg of my deaf child. I must do this to save you. To save our family farm and to spare my only brother's life, I must drink the mushroom brew. To avenge the lives that Valdis has taken, and to halt the deaths she plans to cause, I must use everything I can to make myself strong.

If we are to survive, I must start and end my war this same day.

I skim the mushrooms out with my fingers, then bring the cup to my lips, taking a long drink. I look down to make sure my curved knife rests in its sheath—the only weapon I need.

I lean against a wall as rage floods me, but I let it pass, waiting for the calming feeling that always chases it away. The bold peace. Lights seem to flutter around me, holding me up.

I drape Ref's cloak about me, pulling the door shut as I walk outside. I slip silently through the wet grass to the Icelanders' longhouse. My bare feet cannot even feel the cold of the melted snow.

In fact, there is only one thing I feel. I feel like a hunter.

TWENTY

A STURDY MAN STRIDES out the Icelanders' longhouse door, leaving it wide open behind him. He doesn't nod to me, but his surly gaze tells me he knows who I am. This early in the morning, he is probably going to catch fish.

I feel I am watching myself from high above as I take one risk after another. Walking into the darkened longhouse. Standing in the center of the room, trying to discern Finnbogi from the bodies lining the benches along the walls. Finally deciding he must be on the far end of the room because I can make out a white-blond head peeking from under a fur pelt. Knowing if I have misjudged and chosen Helgi instead of his kinder brother, I will probably be cut down by the entire crew on the spot.

Finnbogi rouses as I tap him, confusion in his eyes. "What do you want here, Freydis?"

I whisper. "I want you to get up and come outside. I have to speak to you."

He pulls on the boots by his bedside and silently follows me out. I sit on a fallen log near the house, motioning him to my side.

I give him a smile that almost feels natural. "How do you like it here in Vinland?"

He gives me a strange look. "If you want to know, I do feel this land has much to offer. But I don't like the ill-feeling between our camps. I don't think there is a reason for it."

I could give him two very good reasons with no hesitation. I could tell him of the murders his wife has committed and her abominable plans for my unborn child.

Instead, I let the mushroom juice work its magic, and I force myself back into a tranquil state. I nearly choke on my words, but I must say them, must convince him I mean him no harm.

"What you say is true, and I agree. And now I will be honest with you. I want to trade ships with you, because your ship is larger."

He begins to protest, and I hold up a hand to silence him.

I continue. "I want to leave this place."

His pale eyes widen and he rubs his white beard, thoughtful. He knows it will please his wife if my crew sails. That would mean his people could take our camp and have more room to settle here.

I lean back. The thin sunlight filters through my hair and dances over my face. I pretend I am in no rush.

"I suppose I can agree to that," he says. "If that will please you."

My heart swells at his humble words. He recognizes that he must please me, even more than his wife. But he has already let his wife run wild, and she is against me. She will not stop until every one of my crew members is dead.

I smile. This is the day I will be free of all of them.

He smiles hesitantly in return, offering his hand. We clasp hands for a moment as a sign of our agreement. He returns to his longhouse and I go down the path to our camp.

Before I open the door of our hut, I pull the silver comb from my hair and run my hands through the curls, making them stand out in all directions. I tuck the pretty trinket into the pocket of my overdress, not caring what happens to it now.

I carelessly open the door, slamming it shut behind me. After taking off my belt, I throw myself into the bed next to Ref, my damp dress clinging to my wet legs and feet. I shove my toes against Ref's legs, and he jumps up.

"What is this? Why are you wet? And you're so cold, you're going to freeze me out of this bed, woman!"

Now is the time. I loose the power of my anger, all the hatred I have built toward this woman who has already taken much and plans to take all. My hands begin to shake and my voice wavers.

"I went to the brothers and asked to purchase their ship since theirs is larger. They became enraged, and they hit me and mistreated me."

I pull up my skirts, revealing the bruise I got from the rocks. It must be large and discolored, because he gasps.

I cannot relent, continuing my tirade.

"And here you sit like a mute, impotent oaf. You are such a coward, you won't repay them for this dishonor they did to me—to you. This is what happens when I am so far from my home in Greenland. I will say this only once: unless you avenge this, I will divorce you!"

His gray-and-white beard flexes with his jaw. His eyes flash. He jumps from our bed, dressing quickly and strapping on his sword. I trail him out the door as he begins to wake the men in each hut. Atli tries to come along, but I force him to stay behind, as he is still not strong enough to fight.

One by one, my men join us, fully armed. The mushroom effects have begun to make me feel strong, as if I could rip someone limb from limb. But a strange voice—maybe my voice? chants over and over, *And now you know your husband loves you.*

Fueled by my husband's love and by my hatred for the murderous cannibals, I walk at Ref's side as we march into the Icelanders' camp. Tyr follows so close behind me, he steps on my heels twice. I turn to scold him but the blaze in his eyes stops me. He knows what we must do, and he is ready.

The man who was gathering fish stands outside, de-scaling his catch. The moment he sees our armed horde, he rushes into the longhouse.

But it is too late. My men plunge through the open door, capturing each person in the house. Thorgrim stands and cuts lengths of rope so my men can bind their hands.

I stand in the doorframe and watch as Tyr goes straight for Valdis, jerking her from the bed and knotting the rope around her pale wrists. He flips her to the floor like a hooked fish on a ship's deck.

As my men continue to tie the Icelanders, Finnbogi shouts, "What is the meaning of this? Haven't I just made a deal with your woman, Ref?"

Hegli glares at his brother. "*What* did you do?"

Ref does not heed them. He assumes they are lying. "Take them out!" he commands.

The men are pushed outside and lined against the wall of the longhouse. I look over their hardened faces. They will not let themselves be afraid, because cowards do not go to Valhalla.

Ref strides out behind the last man. "What shall we do with them?" Even in this final moment, he is uncertain of taking authority.

I do not hesitate. "Kill them all."

TWENTY-ONE

I SHUT MY EARS to the screaming as the Icelanders are attacked. My men take their lives quickly, with a sword-thrust to the heart, or an axe-chop to the neck.

When they are all dead, lying in their own blood, my husband turns to me. "What of the women? They remain inside. Shall we take them into our camp?"

Narrowing my eyes, I give a short, mirthless laugh. "No. Leave them to me."

I reach for my sword, but realize I forgot to pick it up. Sometimes the mushrooms make me overlook the most important things.

But there is no need to return for it. "Hand me an axe," I say.

Tyr steps forward, blood dripping from his war hammer. He pulls his sharp hand-axe from his belt. There is a question in his eyes. I shake my head. Although he has every right to slay her, it would seem cowardly for him to kill an unarmed woman.

I will save him from the dishonor. My men will not try to stop me.

Gripping the iron-wrapped handle, I step into the cool darkness of the room. Two of the women are already screaming, but Valdis stands tall, a heavy Thor's hammer pendant hanging from her neck.

I walk straight to her and yank on her white-blond braid, forcing her to bow her head before me. "Thor will not save you now."

My arms seem to move of their own accord, sweeping out before the four women who stand in a huddle. "You have been accused of beheading a man and a woman and eating their flesh. We have witnesses. I am certain this is punishable by death in Iceland, and it will be the same fate for you here."

Warmth courses through my veins, and my breathing becomes shallow. Sweat beads on my forehead, even in the chill of the morning. I fix on Valdis' green eyes. "Did you weave this fate, *volva*? I believe Odin has conspired against you."

Quickly, I knock the first woman to the floor, taking the wide, sharp point of my axe and driving it into her throat. Even as her eyes lose sight, I do the same to the next woman, and the next, until only Valdis is left standing.

She spits on my shoe and calls down curses on me and my family. "You will never succeed. The truth will come out and it will kill you, Freydis Eiriksdottir. You godless *forest child*."

The peculiar mix of anger and peace rushes through me, and lights blink on the edge of my vision. My hands swing over my head, gripping the axe. When I look down, Valdis lays at my feet, her fair head cleaved through.

I become aware of Tyr, standing behind me in silence. "We are avenged," I say.

The giant man pats my blood-spattered back. "We are safe," he says. "Suka would want you to be safe."

I step outside, joining my silent men. They have shown their loyalty today. Ref comes to my side, sliding his arm around my waist. My vision is strange and my head aches, but I am able to speak. To lead.

"When we make it back to Greenland, if we are fortunate enough to do so, no one will ever speak of the events of this day. If you talk about them or even hint at them, I will have you killed. We have one story to tell: the Icelanders decided to remain behind when we sailed."

My men murmur their agreement. It will be an easy enough tale to tell my brother. He will not care about the Icelanders, just about the plunder I can bring him. I grimace as I think of Valdis' plans to take over Brattahlid. Leif can never know of them, of what happened here, but I wish he could be aware of the risks I have taken today—for him, and for my own child. For our family.

I tell my men to pile the bodies by the shore and burn them there. Ref helps me stumble back to camp. I pull my hand from his, although I do not want to. I have one final command.

"You must tell Kitta they are all dead." I cannot bring myself to look at the girl's face.

In the night, even as he sleeps, Ref's palm lies on my forehead, like a blessing. He never questioned my command to kill the Icelanders when they were defenseless. He never asked why I killed the volva. He never asked how I had the strength to cleave Valdis' skull, although I am sure Gudrid has told him of my past use of mushrooms.

My father used to say "A man's own hand is most to be trusted." At the end of this day, which is the end of a war, I begin to doubt the truth of this proverb.

My husband's strong hand has always been welcoming, always protective. Always to be trusted.

My own hands are now covered in blood that will never wash away.

I lean into his palm, trying to quiet the screams of the women I have killed.

PART TWO

Sea Voyage and Settling at Brattahlid, Greenland

Circa AD 1001

TWENTY-TWO

WHEN THE TREES BEGIN to bloom, we load the larger ship for our return journey. After much wrestling in my own mind, I have decided to leave the smaller ship here, so it looks as if the Icelanders have chosen to stay. I hate that we will have to leave some of our wood planks and goods behind, but there is no other way.

Tyr will check on the camp and ship from time to time, but he has made the decision to move back to his wife's family, to protect her people in honor of her memory. He has no wish to return to Greenland. I have hope he will take another Skraeling wife, who will ease his many sorrows.

Loading is not easy with my stomach that stands out like whale blubber, but I will not be slack in my duties, even though the babe will come soon. The child seems to move about like a great walrus, twisting and shoving my insides around. I talk to it every day as I go about my work, and Ref croons over it at night.

Our plunder is substantial. The ground has thawed and we were able to lift grape vines, as well as wheat seeds. Ref has searched for wood that is unique to Vinland, and we have stockpiled that in the

Icelanders' longhouse. Kitta has chosen berry plants to take and I have many animal skins from my hunts.

One thing I have not gathered, nor will I ever touch again: mushrooms. My berserking days are over.

One bright morning, after a solemn goodbye from Tyr, we set sail. Ref wants me to lie around during this voyage, but he knows there isn't a chance I will do that. I will spend my days at the steering-board, or giving commands for the ship's sail.

Atli is back to full health and treats me like a conquering hero. On the deck of our *knarr*, wide though it is, I quickly feel trapped as the boy follows me everywhere. "Like a pup," Ref jokes.

I tell him how to climb the mast in case our sail becomes entangled. After many attempts, his leather boots continue to slide down the smooth wood. He cannot understand how to hold his footing.

"Like this," I finally say. Because I am wearing my husband's belted trousers and a leather vest over a wool tunic, I am able to move easily. I slide off my boots and pull myself up the pine-tarred mast until I am halfway to the top.

The men have started to stare. Ref comes into view and shouts, obviously upset. He should not try to stop me. I climb until I can touch the wooden crossbar at the top of the sail, gripping the mast with the soles of my feet. It is not so hard when you are familiar with it, like climbing a tree with no limbs. Of course, the babe makes it unwieldy, but not impossible.

When I return to the deck, my men clap and Atli bows. "You must be a goddess," he breathes reverently.

I laugh and ruffle his blond hair, although now he stands a hair taller than I do. In just a year or two, he will probably become as large as Tyr. His sword skills have grown, along with his hunting abilities. I know Leif will want to claim him as his own slave, but I have decided Atli will stay at my smaller farm until I can take over Brattahlid. The boy could have become another of Valdis' casualties if she been allowed to continue her murderous schemes. But he has survived, and he will be a boon to my family.

Kitta has watched me in silence for months. She dutifully prepares our crew's meals over a protected cook-fire and checks me faithfully to be sure the babe is in the right position. But there is no trust in her eyes. I cannot sleep, imagining that she watches me at night, her uncanny eyes boring into my head through the leather covering of my sleep sack.

But I have to trust her, because my baby will come soon.

Several days into our voyage, the favorable winds shift. With some maneuvering, I am able to keep the sail positioned so that we do not veer far off-course.

But soon gray clouds bank above us, threatening to burst with storm. Knowing the height of waves we can encounter this far from land, I call on Thorgrim, my water bailer. "Be prepared to do your work, and gather two other men to help."

The men take up their large wooden buckets—buckets it would be difficult for me to lift. At my command, the men pull the oars, flipping built-in wooden coverings into place over the holes to prevent extra water on the deck.

"Should we take down the sail? Looks to be a violent storm," Ref says, even as thunder rumbles in the distance.

I sniff at the charged air. Ref is right. This is no ordinary storm. The babe kicks at me, as if sensing the danger and giving me warning. Even in the womb, my child is a true sailor.

Although I would prefer to leave the sail in place, we have no horsehair to make more rope, should one of our sail riggings snap. Also, there would be little hope of repairing the striped wool sail, which must have involved weeks of work for the Icelandic women.

"Take it down," I say.

My men scramble at the ropes, even as the skies open with rain. Lightning flashes as they wrap the sail, slowly placing it lengthwise along the center of the ship.

Sharp fingers of pain tear through my sides, forcing me to cry out. Dagmar pokes her head out from the blanket she's huddled under.

"M'lady?"

"Find…Kitta!" I shout.

I flail my hands around, trying to capture Ref's attention, but he stands at the opposite end of the ship, directing the men, and he can't see me in this downpour. I sink to the deck, hoping someone will realize I am not manning the steering-board.

Kitta notices before Dagmar's slow steps can reach her. She speaks to Ref, then skirts over the sail and around the men to reach me. Huld appears, dragging a sopping wool blanket she tries to set up over me as a tent. The blanket dumps more water on me than the open rain, and Kitta yanks it off.

She barks orders at the old women, sending them scurrying. She speaks in a low voice to me. I can only hear some of her words above the ripping wind, but I understand that she wants me to tuck closer into the ship's side, in an attempt to avoid the water sloshing onto the deck.

Between pains, I scuttle into a nook, and Kitta promptly covers me with a dry blanket. Beneath it, her nimble hands work quickly to first remove my boots, then Ref's trousers. I have a strange sensation and water spills onto the deck below me.

She leans toward my ear so I can hear every word. "It is coming. You must push when the babe tells you to push."

The blanket begins to smother me, but when I pull it off my head, water spills directly into my mouth, gagging me. Atli rushes to pick up a corner of it and someone takes the other side, holding it aloft as Kitta's cold hands touch my thighs. I glance to my left, making out Ref's boots as he stands at the steering-board. I feel a small measure of comfort, knowing my husband is not far off.

Suddenly, the pressure becomes so intense, I must yield. I strain to push my child into the world, but when the pressure drops off, Kitta urges me to wait. After several other starts and stops, I can no longer hold back, screaming as I push with everything inside me.

I feel a sweet release. The babe has slipped from my body. But this is not the first child I have given birth to, and I fear seeing the end result of this labor. What if it is another blue, limp babe? What if I have failed again to become a mother?

The ship rocks under me and I watch Ref's boots approach. He pulls the blanket from my head, draping it over my waist. I close my eyes, unwilling to watch his open heartache if the babe is dead.

But a cry rends the air, a loud mewling like a baby lamb or bird.

The bold cries do not stop, even as the water slams into us here on this open deck.

I open my eyes and look down. Kitta crouches, holding my flailing babe. She wraps it in cloths, then carefully passes the swaddled body to me.

Ref leans in to touch first the babe's wet red hair, and then mine. "A girl, she said."

I pull the cloths down and take in the closed eyes, the tiny pink mouth that opens and closes like a fish. The babe is alive. She is mine.

When her tongue protrudes, I latch her onto my breast, ignoring Kitta's firm pushes on my stomach to remove the afterbirth. The rain continues to sweep over us, but I can only feel the warmth of my baby's weight on my chest. I share a smile with Ref, floating on a cloud of newfound joy.

I grip her tightly. "My daughter."

TWENTY-THREE

ONCE THE STORM IS behind us, we make remarkable time. The winds favor us and push the knarr at her top speed. Atli knows the constellations, so he makes sure we stay on course at night, and during the days, I watch the sun's shadow, whale feeding areas, and bird formations for confirmation of our route.

My girl stays with me at all times, secure in a wool sling Kitta has tied around my shoulders. It is easy for me to stand by the steering-board with her, so I don't slack in my duties. Ref takes over when I need to feed the baby.

She drinks heartily, as if she can't get enough milk. I am surprised I can make enough for her, because I have always been so thin.

Ref pushes me to decide on a name, but I am unsure. I will not give her the name of a goddess. And Gudrid's name has already been taken by one of my brother's children.

As I look into her steel-blue, guileless eyes, I think of what I want for my daughter. I want her to learn to fight, to hunt. But I also want her to be more giving than I am, more capable of showing love. Most of all, I want her to have what every Viking woman needs:

courage. I decide on *Amoda*, because it can mean courage and because I love the warm sound of it.

It is clear she is not Suka's child. Her features are very nearly a copy of my own, her wisps of hair are red, and her skin is white as snow. I am strangely saddened that I have no reminder of Suka, but I know it is for the best. Ref can love her as his own, with no hint of scandal. She is not a forest child.

Shore-birds begin to swirl about our ship, and land comes into view. I can't begin to hope it is Eiriksfjord, but it might be close enough we can weigh anchor, then travel by horse or on foot to Brattahlid.

My men row into the tight fjord, and I recognize the jutting white cliff we glide past. I gasp in disbelief. We are not far from home.

Ref clasps me around the waist, encircling Amoda as well. She smacks her lips and tries to focus on him.

"You are a good mother," he says.

I meet his earnest gaze. "Perhaps you are surprised?"

"Not at all." He kisses my cheek, then takes the steering-board.

Kitta moves about the deck, serving the men dried jerky for their meager mid-day meal. Both Dagmar and Huld have become sick and cannot stop coughing, so they are resting in their sleep-sacks.

Once again, I notice how the men cannot keep their eyes from Kitta. Her cloud of black hair, unbraided and long, falls in soft waves around her face. Her laugh comes easily in response to their endless teasing. When Thorgrim lazily thumps her backside, I stride over.

"Kitta, please step closer."

Her ocean-blue eyes take on a teary sheen. Is she so upset by Thorgrim's boldness? Or is she more fearful of me?

I pull my curved knife before she can run. Thorgrim's gaze moves from the knife to the girl and back to me. He does not make a move to intervene.

Snatching a handful of her smooth hair, I slide my knife along it in a straight line, chopping off half an arm's length. I toss the dark heap overboard, and Kitta's tears begin to spill. Silence cloaks the deck, occasionally broken by the rhythmic clunk of the oars and Kitta's gasping sobs.

Why must I always go about things the wrong way? I didn't mean to break her, only to protect her.

I try to pat her arm, but she yanks it away from me. Ref strides across the deck, but instead of aiding me, he wraps his strong arm around Kitta's shoulders and shoots me a glare.

"Why do you torment the girl?"

His unexpected gruffness takes me aback, but I quickly recover. "She is no *girl*, Ref. She is a woman, and she must be careful around my crewmen."

Atli has come to my side, watching in silence. I appreciate his quiet presence, but perhaps he thinks I have done wrong, too.

Kitta's sobs grow stronger, as if she's crying out all the hurts she has experienced in her short lifetime. Atli surprises us all by taking her hand in his and leaning in earnestly toward her face.

"I believe m'lady was concerned for your safety, just as she will be for her own daughter someday." At my encouraging nod, he continues. "It's true, I've heard these men talking at night, and there's no doubt you're lucky you've made it this far without being ravaged. Perhaps if you hide your hair you will seem more like one of the crew."

This is exactly what I was thinking, but couldn't put into words. Atli is a good spokesman for me.

"Yes." Amoda is restless and I bounce her in my arms to calm her. "I did not mean to frighten you, but soon we will arrive in Brattahlid, and my brother is like one of the ice bears, prowling for women now that his wife has left him."

I glance at Ref, and he drops his arm, finally believing I mean the girl no harm. He gives me one final disappointed glance, then returns to take the steering-board from Bork.

Kitta snuffles loudly, but even red-faced and bleary-eyed, with her hair cropped around her slightly-pointed chin, she is beautiful. Like Gudrid, her beauty will likely be the heaviest burden she will carry in life.

I turn my back to her tears. Positioning myself on one of the higher chests, I pull Amoda from her sling. She pushes toward me, hopeful for another feeding. I pull down my overdress and shift, tucking her close so she can eat. "My brave baby girl," I murmur. "You wouldn't cry if your *modi* cut your hair, would you?"

The rowing slows and I look up, amazed to see the shoreline coming up fast. Ref skillfully stays in the deepest part of the fjord until we can slide close enough to drop anchor. Horses graze near the water's edge, and several men stand on the rocky sand, ready to greet us.

Probably shepherds, I tell myself. Or slaves, looking for some excitement.

As we draw closer, a tall blond rides up and pushes his way forward. He shouts something I can't make out.

But I know who it is. Returning a satiated Amoda to her sling, I stand and wave with more heartiness than I feel.

My brother has come to greet me. I can only hope my plunder will inspire Leif to forgive me for stealing away with half his slaves.

Someone else stands on shore, her purple overdress skirt dancing on the light breeze, her blonde hair twisted high on her head. A small boy stands at her side, gripping her hand. Her stomach is large with child. My heart leaps as I recognize the only woman who has ever been a friend to me.

Gudrid is still at Brattahlid.

TWENTY-FOUR

REF DROPS OUR SMALL boat and rows us to shore. He won't meet my eyes, and I fear he won't meet Leif's, either. Instead of acting like the free man he is, he's behaving like a runaway slave.

I won't have it.

I shove his chin upward before we secure the boat, forcing him to look at me even as Leif strides our way. "Don't betray me," I whisper.

Leif leans over to take my hand. From his thick leather vest to his sealskin boots, my brother gives the impression of wealth. His hair and beard are meticulously combed. He stares at my girl and I am unsure what to say.

"You had a child?" He pulls me to my feet, surprise etching his features.

"Indeed." I step toward him, and although he hesitates, I pull him into a hug. My arms don't quite wrap around his huge chest. "How are you, my brother?"

Gudrid edges closer, and I catch a glimpse of my other sister-in-law, Stena, close on her heels. Stena's children frolic around the beach like puppies. I forget how many she has, but I should try to know them better, because her husband Thorvald was my favorite brother.

Leif pulls my attention back. "How am I, sister? Let me think. Brattahlid is operating with half its slaves, Mother has died, and Thorfinn is leaving soon."

His joking tone doesn't cover the spite beneath the words. He locks his hands on my arms, waiting for my response. When his gray eyes narrow, I can tell he wishes he could shake me senseless.

Ref stands helpless at my side. He would never go up against my powerful brother.

I do not give way. "I am sorry for taking your slaves, but the Icelanders would not sail if I didn't have a full crew." Leif sputters, but before he can voice his anger, I continue. "I didn't want the Icelanders to take all the plunder, so I had to go along. And look!" I gesture toward the ship. "I have brought every slave back, as well as a large ship-full of goods."

As he turns toward the ship, Gudrid slides between us, deftly pulling me from Leif's grasp. She kisses my cheeks and Amoda's head. Her son, Snorri, dances around my skirts, hoping for a closer glimpse of the baby.

"You have given birth," she says, her grass-green eyes brimming.

I clasp her hands tightly, unwilling to be torn from this woman who somehow anchors me. I have so much to tell her, yet I can tell her nothing at all. Would she understand why I had to kill the volva?

Stena tiptoes closer, and when I see her smooth, tan face, with those dark eyes of her native Sami people, I choke back a cry. It could have been her head in that hole, if Valdis had come here. She would not have tolerated the presence of one Skraeling.

I have done the right thing.

We embrace, then walk toward the horses as the men speak on shore. "How did you know we were here?" I ask.

"Hellir came to tell us. He was passing by and saw the knarr," Gudrid says. She motions to the dark-skinned boy frolicking with Stena's children. I had nearly forgotten that Gudrid herself had adopted two native boys named Hellir and Hol on our return voyage from Straumsfjord. That makes two more Skraelings I have saved from Valdis. Perhaps Atli could train them at swordplay or hunting.

Gudrid looks me over, then pulls me close. She sniffs hesitantly, then smiles. "You smell clean."

I laugh. "I have decided to take care of myself for the baby—her name is Amoda."

"Little Moda," Gudrid murmurs, touching the red fuzz on my daughter's head.

Kitta falls into step behind us, and Gudrid arches an eyebrow. She waits for me to explain.

"This is an Icelander. I brought her with us because of her birthing skills." I touch Gudrid's large stomach. "Perhaps she will need to help you soon?"

"Indeed. Finn wants to sail soon to Norway for trading, but I believe I have convinced him to wait until I have this child. I do not want to give birth on a ship."

I point to Amoda. "It can be done."

She gasps. "She was born on the knarr? At sea?"

"In a storm," I add.

Gudrid squeezes my arm. "You are a child of strength and fury. And we wouldn't want you any other way."

Leif welcomes us into his imposing longhouse at Brattahlid for the evening meal, although he still openly sulks.

He sits at the head of the table, sipping mead from one of his mother's Rhine-glass cups. His eyes become misty. "My mother had such a difficult time at the end. I was thankful that Gudrid stayed to help, along with Stena, of course." Sniffing, he drops his hand over Gudrid's, since she sits at his right side.

I watch Gudrid's husband, Thorfinn Karlsefni. The man does not tolerate fools, and I know he sees through my brother's exaggerated sorrow. I am quite sure these two leaders have clashed in the months we were away. No wonder Thorfinn wishes to sail for Norway as soon as possible. I see the dangerous glint in his steely eyes, and a shiver of recognition runs through me. Thorfinn hates Leif as I hated Valdis, which means he would not hesitate to kill him.

Gudrid draws her hand away and continues eating her salted pork as if nothing has happened. This is not the first time Leif has touched her so openly. Why can't he set his sights on an unmarried woman, instead of nursing this old affection for a woman who no longer loves him?

Thorfinn turns to me, and I'm struck again by the raw power this man exudes. It's a natural power, not an affected one maintained by force, like Leif's. Perhaps this is why Gudrid overlooks Leif's advances—she knows her husband will protect her.

"I saw the wood you brought back, Freydis. Quite impressive. I'm surprised you were able to talk Helgi into trading ships—he struck me as a greedy man."

A greedy man who would have taken over Brattahlid, given half the chance. "Finnbogi was more willing than his brother," I say, allowing a piece of soft cheese to melt on my tongue. How I have missed rich foods!

Kitta comes over to the table, her short dark hair caught back in a band. She hands me Amoda. "I believe she needs to be fed, m'lady." My daughter gives one loud cry, as if in agreement.

Leif watches the girl for one moment, then his gaze shifts back to Gudrid. I suppose he does not find Kitta attractive, which is comforting. Perhaps I won't have to watch over the girl so closely.

Stena reaches for Amoda as I push back my chair. She begins to croon over her.

I stretch and turn to Leif. "We will stay over tonight, I suppose?"

Leif offers a false smile. "Of course. We have enough room. My slaves' beds have sat empty all these months. It is time they were filled again." He grips his fork in both hands, as if he wants to break it in two.

I glance down at Atli, who is deep in conversation with one of Thorfinn's men. Should I tell Leif I am keeping Atli, or just take him with me when we leave for my farm in the morning? And when can we discuss my intention to buy Brattahlid?

"We need to talk, brother," I say.

Ref leans in close to my side, as if preparing for a blow.

Sure enough, Leif does not disappoint. He jumps from his chair, his hands clenched into fists. "We will not *talk* about my slaves, sister. I will have them back. I paid for each one."

The longhouse falls silent as the men gape. Three groups of men—Leif's, Thorfinn's, and mine. Nearly everyone carries a weapon of some kind. If I do not calm my brother down, this longhouse could turn into a battlefield.

Trying to ignore Amoda's frantic cries, I remain standing. I fight the wild desire to jump onto the table, putting my curved knife to Leif's thick throat until he gives me what I want.

I force myself to bite out the words. "Of course your slaves will stay here. I will only keep one slave in return for the plunder I will give you."

His gaze darts around, as if he's trying to make sense of what I said.

"You are giving me plunder?"

If it means I'm buying the farm, then yes.

"Some of it." I try not to promise things. "I will only take the boy—Atli. I know you thought he could be a warrior, but his sword skills are a clumsy disgrace. It will take many hours to train him. I am doing you a favor by feeding the worthless oaf. But Ref thinks of him as a son, so I will keep him."

I don't meet Atli's gaze, but I know he watches me, as does Ref. My lie is great, but I have told greater. I doubt my husband is shocked, but I hope Atli will forgive my public humiliation.

Leif rubs his beard. Finally, he returns to his chair and shouts over the cries of my baby. "We will talk on this later. But I can't feed any hangers-on here, so you can have the boy. You know my wife took my valuable things when she left."

Actually, she ran away. To another country.

I smile, taking Amoda into my arms. Her screaming stops immediately. "Thank you for the meal, Leif. Father and Thjodhild would have been proud you are keeping the farm up so well."

"My mother..."

I walk out before Leif can describe the sad death of his mother. The woman was barely a mother to me, so I cannot share his loss.

Ref follows me. He says nothing, but wraps his cloak around me in the chilly air. The darkening sky is pricked with countless stars, and I can see the milky green start of the lights that will dance across it. I breathe in the muddy, fresh scent of buds and spring.

It is good to be home.

TWENTY-FIVE

WE SETTLE IN AT my smaller farm, just three fields away from Brattahlid. Ref sets about building bed frames and carving ship figureheads with the Vinland wood. He will sell them for a nice profit.

For now, we all sleep in the longhouse, but soon Ref will need to build a hut for Atli and one for Kitta. Amoda sleeps next to me, in the ornate cradle that was mine as a baby. Though she is a sound sleeper, when she wakes, she rouses everyone with her cries. In my mirror, I see the deepening black circles under my eyes.

Not three weeks pass before Kitta is called to Brattahlid to aid Gudrid with her birth. I ride over later to see her newborn—a plump, rosy-cheeked boy they have named Bjorn.

"Soon you will have your own little horde," I say. "Four sons already."

Gudrid sits on her large bed, nuzzling Amoda. Deirdre, one of her older freed slaves, rocks Bjorn to sleep.

Gudrid flips her long blonde hair away from her face. "I hate to sail from my nieces. Little Gudrid sticks to me like a shadow."

Stena appreciated Gudrid's help with her birth so much, she named her daughter after her. I doubt my family will ever give me a namesake. If I am remembered at all, it will probably be for all the wrong things.

As I relax in Gudrid's hut, my senses are assaulted in a good way. The warmth of the fire, the smell of dried lavender hanging from the beams, and the velvet-covered chair beneath me work together to lull me into a state of complacency. I look directly at Gudrid, her clear green eyes practically forbidding me to tell untruths. Even though she now worships the white Christ, she has always had something supernatural, almost magical, about her.

"You have something you need to tell me," she says.

I turn away, focusing on Thorfinn's sword on the wall. "Why do you say this?"

She laughs. "I know you very well, Freydis—perhaps better than you know yourself. You are happy to be back in Eiriksfjord, happy to be a mother, but there is a new darkness that clings to you like a heavy cloak." She pauses, shifting Amoda in her arms, then her voice hardens. "Tell me you have not been eating mushrooms."

"Not for a while."

"What happened in Vinland, then?" When I remain silent, she leans forward and whispers, although I am sure Deirdre will hear her every word. "Did you try to find Suka?"

Deirdre cocks her head. That Irish slave has always been an eavesdropper, and she cares as little for me as I do for her. Still, I doubt she would report to Leif, since she's loyal to Gudrid.

"Suka found me."

Gudrid twists her lips, unsure. I know she is envisioning the day he tried to attack her at Straumsfjord. "Was he well?"

"He was. Tyr came too. He settled with a Skraeling wife." I must stop talking.

"And was Suka…happy?"

While Suka was recovering from his wolf-bite injuries, Gudrid had told him about her God. I recall what he told me and try to choose my words carefully.

"He is at peace."

Gudrid gives me one long look, then nods.

"And your Kitta, how is she? She is a gifted birther. Perhaps she misses her Icelandic friends?"

I must escape these pointed questions. Gudrid will drag the truth out of me yet.

Bjorn begins to cry, and I jump up, nearly snatching Amoda from Gudrid's arms so she can feed her own child. She narrows her eyes.

"You are not telling me something, Freydis Eiriksdottir."

I glance at Deirdre, who seems to wear a mask of boredom. I cannot risk speaking in front of her.

"Someday we will have more time to talk," I say.

"Not soon! Finn is readying our ship. You know we must sail tomorrow."

Rocking Amoda in my arms, I must ask one more question of the woman who knows my brother best. "You have seen the plunder I have. Do you think Leif would sell me Brattahlid?"

She gasps. "You want to buy the farm? But he is the eldest—"

"Father would have wanted me to run it. You know this."

"I am not sure, Freydis. Eirik loved you both. He would not have wanted you to fight over it."

I clench my jaw. "You are blinded by Leif. Do you still think him such an admirable man, after living near him for months? Surely he has tried to take advantage of you."

She shakes her head. "Never, not after...he would not try anything. Yes, his eyes follow me everywhere, but he would not cross Thorfinn."

Perhaps she is right. Leif looks at Thorfinn the way a beaten wolf eyes the pack leader.

I turn to go, but Gudrid's melodic voice reaches me at the door. "Will you not say goodbye?"

I do not want to fare her well; I do not want to say goodbye. I would rather walk out and pretend I could come to this hut and talk to her any time I want.

I face the door instead of looking back at her. "Our children won't be together." My voice wavers in a way I despise.

The bed shifts. "Perhaps they will. I will not soon return to Brattahlid, but you must come to me when we are settled in Iceland. Promise you will. I will send a messenger when we are safely there."

She has drawn closer, stepping up behind me and laying her hand on my shoulder. I finally turn into her open arms, our babies touching. The next time they meet, they might be walking. She pats my head as I let out a gasping cry, wishing I could weep out all the bitterness of my soul.

"You have seen too much, Freydis, and shouldered too heavy a load. Let Ref help you," she murmurs.

After several moments, I am able to leave her. Even as I walk toward my farm, her words burn in my mind: *let Ref help you.*

If only I knew how.

TWENTY-SIX

One Year Later

MIST HAS COATED THE forest where I track a small herd of reindeer. This time of year, the damp leaves are silent, giving me an advantage. When I have a clear view of the larger bull, I swiftly place my arrow's notch into the bowstring and release it.

The animal drops and I wait a moment before approaching. We will have fresh meat tonight—softened reindeer is Amoda's favorite. And Leif should appreciate my effort because he does not hunt often, and his slaves are not skilled at hunting, either.

I work to gut the animal before slicing it into large pieces I can drag along in my leather sack. When I add the salmon and fresh peas I gathered yesterday, we will have a good offering to bring home tonight.

Home to Brattahlid.

I can't hold back my smile, still awed that I own half my family farm. Not only do we have our own longhouse, but Atli and Ref have built huts for all of us.

Tonight I will speak with Leif about buying more of the farm. I finally have an advantage I can use—the Vinland grapevines we will soon plant. I can almost see his mouth watering as he thinks of the wine he could make and sell with his own vineyard.

This past year, I have hunted and trapped to provide for Leif's servants. I have sold my smaller farm and given Leif all the profits. I have helped Stena go through Thjodhild's luxuriant clothing, ordering my women to sew new dresses, trousers, and tunics with the cloth.

Anyone with eyes can see that I have made myself like one of my brother's slaves.

Ref does not like this. He itches for more privacy and frequently mentions our old farm.

"We would have more food if we didn't have to serve your kills to Leif's men," he will say. Or, "Dagmar and Huld are nothing but skin and bones. Your brother refuses to feed them enough."

While these things are partly true, I cannot seem to convince Ref to take a longer view. If I sacrifice for Leif now, will he not reward me with more in the future?

Ref meets me outside our hut. He takes my heavy bag and hauls it into the longhouse for me. Each time I return from my hunts, I always ask the same question.

"How is Amoda?"

"She has eaten and probably plays with Kitta." He lays out the meat haunches on the table.

Ref has whittled and polished so many toys for Amoda, the girl will never lack for something to do. Kitta's hut is full of her treasures.

"I will go to her," I say.

Ref's intense gaze rakes over my body. "You are covered in blood. Perhaps you should bathe first."

I hear the meaning behind his words: he wants me to clean myself so he can be close with me tonight. I cannot deny that since Amoda's birth, we have had little time together. Even now, she wakes frequently and I have to place her between us for nursing. And I have been too busy working for Leif's benefit to pay attention to what I look like. Today I wear the same shift and overdress I have worn all week.

Yet anger flows through me because Ref does not understand or support what I am doing for us, for our children and grandchildren. I am trying to take over Bratthlid, and he seems to want no part of it. He refuses to help Leif and focuses only on carving things for our own profit.

I whirl away. "I will see my daughter, blood or no blood."

───※───

When I step into Kitta's bright hut, which is well-lit with two window openings she insisted on having, I am confused. Amoda sits alone, far too close to the fire. As I step into the room, she drops her wooden horse and walks toward me, her unpracticed gait halting.

"Kitta?" Sweeping Amoda into my arms, I peer under her bed, but there is no one else in the room. I throw her door open, shouting louder. "Kitta?"

Irritation and fear battle for my thoughts. Is the girl hurt, or has she just become lazy? If she cannot watch Amoda while I hunt, I may have to buy one of Leif's slaves.

Seeing nothing, I return to the longhouse. Ref stands in the back corner, oblivious to the flies swirling around the meat. He is deep in conversation with Kitta.

She wears a red wool overdress, along with milliflori beads and an embroidered belt. With her dark hair swept into a high knot woven through with a thin golden band, she looks as if she could be a jarl's wife.

I wish I could cut her hair off again.

I stalk up to them and shove her shoulder. "Explain to me why you left Amoda in your hut alone."

Ref's eyes widen and he turns back to her. "You did not leave her with Dagmar?"

Kitta smoothes her pale hands over her dress. "I had no time. Leif came for me and wished to talk."

I can only imagine why—he must have set his sights on her. Maybe I could trade her for one of his slaves.

"He is interested in you?"

She drops her eyes and does not answer. Perhaps she is embarrassed at my brother's advances. Perhaps he did not want to make her his wife, just his lover.

I turn to my husband. "And what do you know about this?"

Ref shrugs, but his eyes are dark as if something troubles him. He does not even answer me. "You need to let Kitta prepare this meat for the meal tonight." He leans over and kisses a wriggling Amoda on her curls, then walks outside to work.

I reward Kitta for her incompetence with a glare that could melt glass, but she still refuses to meet my eyes. I don't have time to sit around asking what Leif wanted. Huffing, I hoist Amoda higher in my arms and stamp out.

Halfway to my hut, I groan. I cannot avoid washing up and changing my clothing for tonight. I must look wealthy, like someone who will be a respectable leader and bring prosperity to Brattahlid.

I cannot look like a forest child.

TWENTY-SEVEN

DAGMAR WATCHES AMODA IN her hut as I dress for the meal. I am thankful Kitta is busy preparing food, because it is safer for her if I don't see her face again today.

I choose a snow-white linen shift, extensively embroidered in yellow. Thjodhild left behind a wine-colored velvet overdress, which has been altered to fit my height, and I slip that on. Three silver strands, heavy with varying sizes of carnelian and jet beads, hook onto my silver brooches. I place three rings on my fingers, one a large ruby Thjodhild left to me.

Huld tries to braid and twist my hair, but the mirror does not lie. My curls fall from their combs in a disarray, making me look as if I just crawled out of bed. Like me, my hair will always do whatever it wants. I yank the combs out and let it fall heavily over my shoulders.

Only my keys and my knife hang from my belt, not my sword. It puts me at a disadvantage, should Leif rise up against me, but he would be ill-at-ease if I brought a larger weapon.

Ref bursts through our door, shedding his dirty tunic and

trousers. Huld keeps her eyes on me, ignoring him as he washes with a cloth. His torso is pale from winter, but his arm muscles are always tight from moving huge pieces of wood. A shiver of desire runs through me, so unusual that it almost feels strange.

Knowing I need my husband's support tonight, I motion Huld out of the hut, then walk to Ref's side. I run my fingers over his bare chest.

"I promise things will be easier if I own a larger share of Brattahlid," I say. "Unlike Leif, I will make sure all the slaves have plenty to eat. Haven't I already helped by hunting?"

Ref sighs. "You cannot take care of everyone, Freydis. You have already helped Leif's slaves who sailed with us to Vinland. They have been able to trade their goods and some have even bought their freedom. You owe them nothing."

A strange coldness edges Ref's gaze. Perhaps it is my fault, for resisting him for so many months, but I sense there is another wedge between us.

I step closer. "Is there something—"

He turns his back to me.

Before I can force him to face me, a knock sounds. My angry stride matches the heat in my face as I throw the door open.

Kitta stands outside, laden with baskets of steaming food. Her gaze is bolder than normal as she meets my eyes. "The food is prepared. We can go now."

I turn to tell Ref, but even as he pulls on his shoes, his gaze is not on me. He watches Kitta, decked in her velvet cape that emphasizes the softness of her features.

Her deep blue eyes flick to his for a moment, almost like a caress. Do they think I am blind?

Atli strides alongside me on the path to Leif's, and I am grateful for his light-hearted chatter. He has learned new spear techniques from Thorgrim, he says. Also, Ref has made him a new shield with a double layer of boards and iron bands. Atli has painted it red and white. His youthful cheeks glow with excitement. He cannot wait to fight in a real battle.

Let us hope that battle won't occur tonight, when my brother hears my request.

Dagmar and Huld have stayed behind with Amoda. I cannot risk having my daughter with me if Leif becomes difficult.

And why should he? I have done nothing but serve the man since I returned, and he must know how that bothers me. It is not in my nature to serve or to be served. I take care of myself, and that is enough.

We top the hill and Leif's longhouse sprawls into view. At least Ref has built me one nearly the same size that is more eye-catching with its heavily-carved beams and doors.

Leif strides out to greet me. He wears red wool leg-wraps, quite showy and unnecessary since the weather is warming. They are of better use when the snow is thick. His blue tunic has wolves embroidered on it, and his leather belt repeats the design. His dark leather shoes are secured with toggles, not laces.

This is what Leif's clothing says to me: he is a wealthy man, a man worthy of owning Brattahlid.

And yet I stand tall, knowing my dress equals his. He looks over my jewelry and clothing, then chuckles and claps several times.

"Freydis Eiriksdottir, if you aim to impress, you have succeeded.

Rarely have I seen you looking this…polished."

My temper flares and I cannot hold back. "Perhaps if I didn't have to ramble everywhere to hunt food for your men, I could idle about as you do."

He smiles, then winks at Ref over my shoulder. I cannot see Ref's response, but I hope it is sufficiently cool.

Leif walks over and takes one of Kitta's food baskets. "Let me help you with this."

I listen for extra softness in his words, but there is no hint of it. Why would Leif have asked to speak privately with Kitta if he is not attracted to her?

As we sit at one of the long tables, Thorgrim catches my eye. He sits in a shadowy corner, which makes his swarthy face look even darker. And yet that flash in his eyes—is it anger? Or fear?

Stena and her active brood sit beside me on the bench. Little Gudrid appears to be a handful, squirming under the table and popping out the other side. Stena clucks and scolds and positions the child back in her seat, where she promptly knocks her small cup over.

As she mops up the spill with a cloth, Stena's soft brown eyes take in my velvet overdress. "It looks perfect on you. Thjodhild would be proud," she murmurs.

I doubt anything I could do would have made my stepmother proud, but I smile nonetheless.

One of Stena's sons gives me a shy smile in return, and I catch my breath. He looks so much like Suka would have as a child—those liquid eyes, that thatch of thick black hair, and that smooth honey skin.

"You have beautiful children," I say.

"They do not resemble their father very much, although little Oivand has Thorvald's eyes."

As usual, the mention of my favorite brother's name hits me like a hammer to the chest. "I am so sorry no one has been able to find his body so it can be returned to Brattahlid. He was always a good brother to me. Perhaps I have avenged him by killing Skraelings who attacked our camp, just as they attacked Thorvald in his ship."

Too late, I remember that Stena herself is considered a Skraeling with her Swedish Sami blood. But she does not flinch. Stena is so slow to speak and react, I wonder if anything would make her flinch.

Instead, her eyes flicker briefly toward Leif, as if comparing the brothers in her mind. Having lived at Brattahlid for a few years, she must have been witness to Leif's moodiness. Her eyes meet mine, a question in them, but Leif's voice spirals louder and he directs a comment toward me.

"I said, how are you enjoying farm life at Brattahlid, sister?"

I hold up a bite of goat cheese, then pop it into my mouth so he can see how I savor it. "Fresh cheese and butter—it is everything I could wish for. I never want to be without cows and goats again!"

"That's right—you couldn't take any animals to Vinland when you ran off on me, could you?" He laughs, but one by one, the men fall silent, sensing the way this conversation could go.

I echo his false laugh with one of my own. "You know I'm not the type to plan."

He narrows gray eyes that are dark as a snow-filled sky, leaning in toward me. "Is that so? Because that is not what I hear."

TWENTY-EIGHT

MY CONFIDENCE WAVERS, BUT I mask it with a smirk. Ref sits across from me, obviously trying to catch my eye, but I won't break my stare-down with Leif.

I try to brush his comment off like an annoying fly. "I don't know what you hear, but it's obvious I left in a hurry to take the Icelanders up on their offer of a ship. I had to have a crew, and I took some of your men, because you wouldn't give me your blessing. And yet look what treasure I have returned with! Look how I have served you endlessly since I have been home! One full year of killing and trapping and bringing food to your table. Have I not been a boon to you, brother?"

Leif pushes his fingers together and props his chin on them, falling silent. His silence is more ominous than an open chastisement.

Everyone focuses on chewing their tender reindeer meat and cheese. The yawning quiet is broken only by little Gudrid, who seems to be fond of her Uncle Leif. She breaks from her seat and rushes to his leg, clinging to it and sticking her tongue out at her mother. Leif pats her head in one of his casual displays of affection.

Memories pour over me without warning. Leif rarely hugged me when we were young. I recall once when we were wrestling, he realized he'd nearly choked me. Rolling off me, he gave me a hug before racing to the longhouse for the mid-day meal.

He hugged me once again when we were older and father told me I couldn't sail to Vinland with the men. Leif actually seemed sorry I couldn't join him, which was a wordless acknowledgement of my sailing and fighting skills. He gave me a brief hug, but it was enough to set off a torrent of tears so strong I clambered up a tree to hide.

And now here I sit, wishing I could cling to my brother's leg like little Gudrid and beg him to give me what I want. If only I could tell him what I have done for him—protecting this farm from the murderous, grasping talons of Valdis. Protecting his slaves from being killed in a surprise attack by the Icelanders. Surely he would understand and turn the farm over to me, as our father wanted.

Instead, when the meal is finished, he says he needs to speak with me. Alone.

As the men file out, Thorgrim bumps into me. When I meet his eyes, he slowly drops his gaze to his arm, where a huge gash lays open. I suck in my breath and reach for Stena.

He shakes his head, jerking it toward Leif.

Something has happened and he is warning me. He fixes his eyes straight ahead and shuffles after the others.

Stena did not see his wound. "What is wrong?"

"You must tell Kitta to look at Thorgrim's arm. He has had an accident."

The kind of accident I might have, the moment I am left alone with my brother.

※

Instead of rushing to my side, as I expect him to do, Ref turns his back to me, helping Kitta with her empty baskets. Watching the way she dips her dark head, raising it so close to his chest, makes me want to scream.

Atli makes his way toward me and I stiffen, trying to funnel my anger into an appearance of strength. My words come out sharper than I intend.

"Find Amoda. Stay with her until I return." I cannot say more, but he understands and nods. The old women will not be able to protect my daughter if Leif decides to send his men over.

I blink as Atli leaves, my gaze falling to my rings, my beads, my velvet overdress…each item an obvious, groveling effort to impress my brother.

Hatred scrapes its way up my body, like a knife stripping a pelt of its flesh. My half-brother does not love me, though we share our father's blood. Perhaps it is time to stop deluding myself, stop trying to appease him. Perhaps it is time to take what I want.

Yet Ref has asked me before, and now I must ask myself—why is it so important that I own Brattahlid? Is it because it meant so much to me as a childhood home? Is it because Eirik the Red taught me here, training me to fight and sail and hunt? Or is it simply because I want to thwart Leif's claim to ownership?

All this tumbles through my head as Ref and Kitta walk out together, fitting through the wide doorframe like one person.

Like any warrior, I bury my raw emotions and channel my rage into a force that would bury me if I couldn't control it. I pull out my curved knife, then slide from my bench and position myself behind Leif's chair. As the last person leaves the longhouse, I press the knife to my brother's throat.

"You have harmed Thorgrim. I want to know why."

The unfortunate thing about brothers is that they know their siblings' weaknesses. Leif's large hand shoots to my side, where he starts up a painful tickling movement that forces me to squirm away.

I drop to the bench, cupping my knife in my palm and trying to shoot arrows at him with my eyes. "I will ask you again—why did you hurt Thorgrim?"

Leif leans back, stretching his long legs as if he has no cares at all. "I am quite sure Thorgrim told you nothing. So where do you get the idea I harmed him?"

I huff. "I am sure he told me nothing because you threatened him not to. Don't be an ogre, Leif. Why harm your own warrior?"

He yawns, enjoying making me wait for his answer.

I form a fist under the table, then ram it into the fleshy side of his knee. He gives a brief yelp, shoving his chair back. I know his weaknesses too.

His eyes narrow. "Since you want honesty, I will be honest with you, Freydis. Someone has told me that the Icelanders will not be sailing anywhere, because they are *all dead*. Indeed, if this story is to be believed, they were all murdered in a cowardly and decidedly un-Christian way. There was no *Althing* called, no laws invoked. They were destroyed without warning."

Anger pulses in my ears. Who has betrayed me?

He reads the question in my eyes. "You know sailors cannot stay silent—they must brag about every conquest. When word of this massacre reached me, you should be thankful I took the time to make sure it was true before accusing you. I have questioned several of your crew members very thoroughly—yes, even your Icelandic beauty, Kitta. Finally, one of them spoke up with the truth, although I will not tell you who. I brought the others back and they had to agree the story was true, down to the last vicious detail."

Thorgrim's arm wound speaks to the type of thorough questioning Leif used. It was torture.

I shudder to imagine what Leif might have done to Kitta. She is not strong enough to hold up to the threat of serious pain. But perhaps she shared my secrets readily—after all, wasn't she tethered to the Icelanders when they sailed? She probably still has some loyalty to them. How much does she truly know about what happened in Vinland?

What hurts the most is that the people I wanted to protect—Kitta, Leif, and perhaps even my own husband—are the ones who turned on me the fastest. Was Ref tortured?

As I think about the way he looked at me earlier, an even more wretched idea grips me: was he the one who reported the truth to Leif?

TWENTY-NINE

EVEN AS I HOLD Leif's disdainful glare, my body begins to shake as I anticipate his pronouncement upon my deeds.

Will he take me to the Althing and denounce me as a murderer? Will he order his warriors—men who were once *my* crew, under *my* command—to hunt down Ref, Atli, and me? Will he demand my child as penance? His only child is across the sea, living with his mother, who is unlikely to ever return to Brattahlid. He needs an heir to run this farm, and he knows my daughter would be capable, if she is anything like me.

Any of these things he could rightfully do. I can only hope that his Christianity will prevent him from taking extreme measures—but hasn't he already taken them by using torture to find answers?

He studies my face, perhaps enjoying my unease. But his face darkens with a look our father used to get when he knew an injustice had occurred.

"You have done wrong, Freydis, and I believe you must know it. You have brought dishonor to our family name. When relatives of the dead Icelanders discover what you have done—and they will, do not doubt it—they will come to Brattahlid for revenge. You have exposed and humiliated us."

I refuse to drop my head or ask for forgiveness. What I did cannot be forgiven, any more than it could have been avoided.

"I accept your blame," I say, meeting his gaze. I will not explain my actions to him, because he will only think I am desperate for his sympathy, offering excuses. I am sure no one who betrayed our tale knew the whole truth—about Tyr's wife, about Suka, about the volva's plans for my child and for Brattahlid. Only Tyr and I knew all the events that led up to the killing, and he is not here to back me.

A surprising softness has crept into his eyes, giving him a vulnerability I have only seen when he is around Gudrid. "I am not the one to deal you the punishment you deserve, sister. But you will not remain at Brattahlid and bring the Icelanders down on our heads. You must move, and far from here."

If I leave, Leif can reclaim the portion of the farm I won at such a high price. The farm I have loved and longed for all my life.

I wrap my arms around myself, trying to calm my increased shaking. "And will you strip me of my ship, as well? It is my only means of escape." Greenland is a trap for me now, with Leif's disfavor following me as clearly as a brand on my flesh.

His gaze trails to the window, as if he could view the sea beyond. The ship would be of great value to him, allowing him to return to Vinland and claim his own plunder. Or he could use it to take his goods to Norway to trade.

He turns to me, and the flash in his eyes tells me he has decided. "If the Icelandic families do come for revenge, they cannot find me with their ship, can they? The knarr is yours. I only hope you can use it to make something of yourself. I am sorry to say it, but I predict nothing but evil will come from your descendants."

As if everything I have done, every sacrifice I have made, is for naught.

Yet he is letting me live. I suppose I should be grateful.

I stand, unable to speak further. If only my brother would embrace me and recall his harsh judgment, I would tell him everything. I would explain why Valdis and all her people had to die, not only to protect our farm, but to protect *him*. I would cry and be more open than I have ever been with him. I would be weak, if only for a moment.

He stands, but he turns his back to me and strides outside, probably returning to his own hut.

In the central hearth, one black coal flickers, then its light dies. Its fire has been used up. Its power is gone.

I smooth the soft skirt of my velvet overdress, then touch the beads that rattle together on my chest. A spot of wine mars the yellow design on my sleeve. My rings feel too heavy. They are nothing but a hindrance for a hunter like me.

I have been lying to myself.

I am no jarl, and I never can be. Leif will not transfer his farm—his inheritance—to me, his half-sister. He will always hold onto Brattahlid, no matter how wealthy I become. He will search for a second wife to bear him another son—a son loyal to him who can take the farm when he dies.

My loyal men have turned on me, shared my secrets with my meddling brother. Perhaps some of the women, as well. Women I have trusted with my daughter's care.

Ref will be thankful we must sail. He will be glad to be free of Leif and his continual demands on me. He will make plans to build a large farm, using his wealth and mine. He will not balk to leave the farm to our daughter, our firstborn.

Perhaps I have not spent enough time with Amoda, thrilling in her trusting eyes that are so beautifully fringed in pale lashes, her long fingers that twine into my hair as she goes to sleep, and her peculiar hum as she plays with toys.

Perhaps this is a chance to be there for my daughter as my mother was never there for me.

For my daughter's future, I will sail.

I destroyed my own future the day I decided to kill Valdis.

In the gray of the evening haze, I nearly trip over Atli where he sits, keeping watch outside the old women's hut. His sword slides into its sheath and he stands to greet me.

"Is all well with Leif? Your daughter is safe inside."

He is so earnest, so loyal, I know he is hiding nothing from me. It is not in his nature to be sly. He is not the one who betrayed me to Leif.

"All is not well, but we will make it so." Thoughts that have been swirling like small fish in the current begin to align. There is but one place I can go, one place I will be able to make a fresh start while maintaining the protection of friends.

"Tomorrow we will sail for Iceland," I say. Gudrid and Thorfinn will be surprised, but they will not turn me away. They know what my brother is like.

Atli does not raise an eyebrow. He simply nods and moves aside so I can gather my daughter. The hut is warm from a fresh-stoked fire, and Dagmar holds Amoda close in a rocking chair, crooning over her pink, sweaty face.

"M'lady." Huld croaks from her bed, where she sits sewing. "No one stopped in while you were gone. You can take the child; she'll likely sleep for a while. She's worn herself out, running to and fro in our little room."

I pull the warm bundle from Dagmar's arms, unable to decide if I want the women to join us on our journey. Did they speak to Leif, weaving a sordid tale of my violence?

I will decide in the morning. They have precious few belongings to pack anyway.

"That is all," I say, noting the women's gaping mouths before I whirl out the door.

Ref will be asleep now, resting before he must plow tomorrow. In the morning, he will be thankful when I tell him we won't have to plant crops for Leif.

I try to push our door open but it is locked. Of course Ref did this, to protect the goods stored in our trunks. Dropping my hand to my belt, I fumble until I find the key that fits the lock. Amoda weights my arm like a sack of oats, but I am able to turn the key and shove the door open with my foot.

The hut is swathed in darkness, save for a small fire in the hearth. I stop, listening for the regular sounds of Ref's breathing, but instead I hear a rustling on the bed followed by an unnatural silence, as if someone is holding his breath.

Has something happened to my husband?

Creeping to Amoda's cradle, I place her in it. Thankfully, Huld was right and she doesn't wake.

I feel for my sword and find it where I left it—hooked on the wall. From there I move swiftly, taking up a torch and shoving its straw into the low fire until it catches.

As the flame sputters to life, pushing the darkness back, and I cast its light over the bed. I grip my sword, ready to plunge it into any stranger who has invaded my home. I nearly stumble over a body on the floor, and I lower the torch so I can see what has happened.

Ref cowers on his hands and knees beside the bed, wearing only his tunic. Relief floods me. My husband is alive. Perhaps I scared him awake and he fell off the bed.

I lightly shove him with the toe of my shoe. "You look like a dog, crouching in the dirt. Did I wake you?"

A slight movement sounds on the bed and I jump, nearly dropping my torch. Someone else is here.

But before I lift the torch to see who hides from me, my heart whispers the truth. Even as I whip the woolen blankets from the huddled figure, my hand involuntarily tightens on my sword.

Kitta lies there, her shift twisted beneath her, her pale, shapely legs exposed. Her black hair floats around her face. When I meet her terrified blue eyes, it is clear how she views me—as a heartless berserker, an avenging valkyrie who cannot be thwarted.

I cannot stay my hand as it draws up the sword, ready to plunge it into a woman who has betrayed me in so many ways.

But Amoda cries out, pulling my attention to her. Ref jumps to his feet, but instead of rushing toward Kitta, begging me to let her live, he moves to comfort our daughter.

He does not love Kitta, or he would have saved her.

My sword drops to the bed and I crumple into a heap. Kitta releases a scream that would wake the souls in Valhalla.

It is time to move on.

THIRTY

AFTER REPEATED ATTEMPTS TO discuss the situation with me, Ref gives up and flings himself onto our bed—the same bed he shared with that thankless pagan. As the night wears on, I can tell from his quick, shallow breaths that he does not sleep, as he pretends to. I nuzzle Amoda into me on our edge of the bed and keep my back to my husband, a man I suppose I hardly know.

How could he keep this a secret? How long has it been going on? How many others know? I have so many questions, but I will not lower myself to ask them, to show I care.

He repeated one statement before I froze him with my wall of silence: "Kitta did not tell Leif of our slaughter."

Does he think that information will procure her safety? Or is he admitting he knows she didn't tell Leif because *he* did?

Regardless who broke under Leif's torture, my husband will learn to live with his guilt.

He has shamed me, shamed the daughter we had together. He has proved I cannot trust him.

Yet as I finally drift toward sleep, he stretches out a hand and rests it on my hair.

I should push it away. But I cannot. It weighs on me with the heaviness of every year of our marriage.

The truth is, I have been clenching something tightly. I've shoved it down so deep, I could not see it growing. A green bud of love for my husband—a bud that was nearly ready to cast off its hard shell and unfurl its petals, softening me, breaking me with a beauty I could not take in.

But forest children are not handed the things they want. They must fight for every favor, knowing each one will slip from their hands soon enough.

I lean into Amoda's curls, taking in the scent of my child, a scent I will recognize my entire life. I may not be able to protect her from everything, but I will protect her from a father who will only embarrass and disappoint her.

Tomorrow, I will sail to Iceland without Ref.

When the sun's beams wake me, a blood-red horizon stretches over the hills. We may run into storms today, but I will have to handle them.

Who will I take with me? I've wrestled with this question all night. Of course, Atli will be by my side. But do I need Dagmar or Huld to watch over Amoda as I guide the ship? And surely I will need some men to row us out of Eiriksfjord. Should I flee with them, or should I ask Leif first? He was willing to give me the ship, if only to save himself from Icelanders' retaliation.

Finally, I decide to take both the old women. They know better than I how much food we will need for our journey, and they can prepare it on board. It will not be as tasty as Kitta's, but I can never see the young traitor again.

Taking Amoda with me, I creep over to Leif's camp, waking Thorgrim and a handful of men who have showed the most loyalty and valor. Many agree to join me and begin to load their trunks.

On my way to rouse Leif, I run into Stena as she carries a basket of clothes toward the creek. Her dark, thoughtful eyes flick from me to Amoda. Intuitively, she kisses Amoda's head, as if for the last time, and draws me into a hug. "Leif has turned you out," she says.

"Yes." My voice cracks and I am unable to speak further.

She does not ask where I am going. Does she fear I will return to Vinland? Or does she guess I will run to Gudrid?

Her warm fingers wrap around my arm. "May you find peace, Freydis Eiriksdottir." As she drops her hand back to the basket, I fight the overwhelming urge to weep for the family I leave behind, for the nieces and nephews I cannot spend time with.

But my murders have spared their lives, and that is enough.

Leif sleeps as he lives—unguarded and confident. His arms and legs sprawl wide and he breathes deeply. I hesitate. Perhaps it is wisest to leave without saying goodbye, without asking for the aid of his men.

Amoda grunts, then squeals, launching toward her uncle as if she knows him; as if he would accept her. As I turn to go, Leif's morning-rough voice stops me.

"You sail today?" He acts surprised, as if he hadn't secretly wished for this.

"Yes. And I would take seven of your men. I will not keep them with me. They can find ways to sail back to you, given their newfound wealth."

He stands, stretching. Amoda gives him an anguished cry for attention. When he steps closer, he catches one of her flailing arms in his hand. She stills for a moment, her eyes fixed on his unruly blond hair. Then she reaches out to grab his beard.

His other hand comes up, and I fear the worst. I yank my daughter back, but not before she tumbles forward, directly into her uncle's outstretched arms. I am shocked into silence when he places a kiss on her wild curls.

"She reminds me of you," he says. "She knows how to get what she wants."

I give a short laugh. I have gotten next to nothing I wanted in life. Leif seems to want me to linger, to reminisce, perhaps. But it is pointless. He has disowned me; he has cursed my descendants, saying nothing good will come of them. A contrary part of me wants to fulfill his curse in the most horrific ways, training up warriors who raid and kill and show no remorse.

But that is not why I fight. I have always fought for my family, my people. And that is what my children will fight for, in their own ways.

Ignoring the wistfulness in his eyes, I snatch Amoda. "Thank you for the men—I will send them back to you straightway after we arrive. Although they may feel more loyal to me, since you tortured them."

I had to give the final cut. It is who I am.

He blinks, sucking in his breath so his chest widens. He is

struggling to stomach my disrespect in the face of his vulnerability.

I hope he cannot stomach it. I hope he remembers the times he preyed on my vulnerabilities—my youth, my dreams—and he chokes on them.

Unable to look at him one more moment, this brother who has always caused me pain, I turn my back and stalk out the door. Amoda's screeching wails trumpet my parting.

THIRTY-ONE

LEIF DOES NOT FOLLOW me, so I assume he went back to sleep. It is not surprising. This day means nothing to him, the day his sister leaves her homeland.

Atli, Thorgrim, and my men are on the rocky shore, loading the ship. I want to delay the inevitable by lending my aid. Yet I know I must tell Ref goodbye. Plodding up the incline toward our hut, I catch sight of him standing outside the door, hands on his hips.

As if I have to answer to him.

He rushes toward us, and Amoda predictably reaches for her father. He sweeps her into his arms and she laughs. She is the only one who can laugh now.

His brow furrows in concentration—he is weighing what to say. Knowing Ref, I imagine he has practiced his excuses. I determine to silence my blistering attacks and give him one last chance to speak. I let myself look full in his eyes one last time, and again experience the wonderment his dual-hued gaze always brings.

His words are not what I expect. "Forgive me. I have always known I do not deserve you."

Nonsense. His wealth has always outstripped mine, until now. He ignores my snarled lip and continues.

"You have the passion of three men. Without your urging, I never would have sailed to the new lands—twice. And I am thankful we did, because now we can settle anywhere. We do not have to live with your brother. Think of it, Freydis—we can choose any land we like."

"How many times have you told me this? The only farm I ever wanted was Brattahlid, and now I cannot have it because *someone* buckled under my brother's half-hearted torture."

He does not refute me. Instead, he takes Amoda's chubby palm and kisses it. She kicks to get down, but he holds her tighter.

"We must make a new start, plant roots elsewhere. Didn't your father do it, all those years ago? He never stayed in one place long."

Ref circumspectly does not mention that my father stirred up trouble everywhere he lived, and that banishment often provoked his relocations.

"Perhaps I am not like Eirik the Red. I want to stay in one place—the place I love."

"Perhaps you could learn to love the place where I am. And your daughter."

"Learn to love? How do you ask this of me, treacherous husband? Why should I give you one drop of love when you bestowed yours so freely on the volva wench?"

He dares to step toward me, eyes pleading. Like a strange dance, I take a step back, waiting for an explanation he cannot give.

"Not everything is a battle," he says.

I level a glare at him.

He makes the mistake of elaborating. "Kitta was soft," he says quietly. "I just needed something soft."

Fury, jealousy, and desire mingle, bubbling up into the venomous words I spew all over him. "Please *do* enjoy your soft and easy women, Ref. Amoda and I are sailing today, so now you will have freedom to do as you like. Build your own longhouse elsewhere in Greenland. If it is a divorce you want, I grant you one. By all means, wed another woman."

I turn at the sound of footsteps behind me. Atli stops short, obviously confused at my words. "Ref is not sailing with us?"

I tamp down my irritation that my young warrior still looks to Ref for some sort of guidance.

"Absolutely not." I grab Amoda and shove past Ref into the cool of our hut, only to be greeted by my husband's familiar scents—cedar, smoke, and salt. I shove my few belongings into trunks, determined to escape. Ref steps in and blocks the door, but I ignore him.

When I finish packing, I take my sword from the wall and place it in its sheath on my belt. I have wrapped my bow in a blanket and carefully packed it, along with my quiver.

As Amoda plays on the floor with a wooden whale Ref carved for her, I am torn between two urges—one, to run full-force into Ref's frame and beat him to the ground, and the other, to kiss him one last time.

He seems to sense my irksome wavering. Taking three strides forward, he pulls me into his arms. His lips cover mine, hungry. Immediately, I picture him kissing Kitta this way, and I shove him back into the wall.

"Stay away from me." My words are loaded with an unspoken threat.

He places a hand on my hip, still possessive and grasping at hope. Again, I imagine his strong hand stroking Kitta's white, youthful skin. I remember how he left me in the woods after our first baby died, how he did not forbid Suka from caring for me. He did not rescue me then, and I know now that he will never rescue me. I will always save myself.

I knock his hand away. "Atli and the men wait for me. I have no time to be idle."

He reaches for me again, but I am tired of this game. I cannot stand his touch. I whirl and pick up Amoda.

"You cannot take my daughter from me," he says.

"There is no time to call an Althing meeting to judge the matter," I reply. "You have done this to our family, leaving me with no choice. Besides, Leif will agree with me, along with his friends. How many friends do you have here in Greenland, Ref?"

It is a harsh blow, but he needs to consider what I say. Ref has made all his alliances based on our family name, not his own.

For a moment, I feel sorry for him. He must stay here as an outcast, at least until he builds or buys a ship of his own. He will miss Amoda, and perhaps he will even miss me.

Then again, he could simply take Kitta as his wife or lover to ease his pain. She is young enough to bear him many children.

I stiffen, forcing myself to look into his unusual eyes. I sever myself from any feeling I once held for him. His eyes hold one last question, but I will not give him time to ask it.

"Atli," I shout, and the boy rushes into our house. "We will load the trunks now. There is no time to lose."

PART THREE

Arrival and Settling in Iceland

Circa AD 1003

THIRTY-TWO

ALTHOUGH IT HAS BEEN years since I have sailed without Ref, I find myself enjoying the voyage to Iceland. Atli keeps me amused with stories of his father's battles, and Thorgrim keeps a sharp rein on the crew. Dagmar and Huld shuffle around in their usual way, but at least they manage to keep food in our stomachs, even if it is not tasty.

I keep Amoda close—most days she stays in the sling on my chest. She longs to run and play, but I cannot risk her toppling overboard. I wish I had a chair with a leather strap on it, such as Ref made for Gudrid's son on our return voyage from Straumsfjord. He was so proud of the carvings he did on that chair, and the way little Snorri fit perfectly into the curve of the seat.

It is pointless to think of such things now.

Still, every day I remember Ref's tormented face when we set sail. It is like one of my mushroom-tainted memories—vividly colored and nightmarish. I wish I could forget how he wailed like an abandoned child, arms outstretched for his daughter.

Leif did not even come to see me off, but Stena and her children did, as well as some of Leif's slaves. As they milled around the shoreline, I caught words the slaves repeated: *murderer* and *cursed*. They wanted me gone from Brattahlid—from my home.

It enabled me to walk away from the farm that had been my childhood dream. I even began to imagine I might never return. I had never been accepted here, and despite my efforts to impress Leif with my wealth and thankless service, I never would be. To Leif, to his people, I was nothing more than a murdering forest child.

As the folding black and green hills of Iceland come into view, my men give a whoop. We will follow the coastline to northern Iceland, where Thorfinn told me his family farm is located. By now, he and Gudrid must have finished trading in Norway and they have probably settled at his homeplace.

I have practiced my story, and I hope Thorfinn and Gudrid will accept it without questioning. I will tell them the truth about Ref—that he shared his bed with Kitta. They will believe I left Greenland to avoid him.

Am I now divorced? I did free Ref in front of Atli, so he would be a witness, but we did not make our decision before a group and we did not divide our property. I have taken off my serpent armband, storing it deep in a chest. I suppose I could now live like an unmarried woman.

Yet I still feel married, and I wonder if I always will.

Once we weigh anchor, we stop at an inn near the shore. I ask the innkeeper about Gudrid Thobjarnardottir, only to receive a blank stare. It is very odd. Gudrid always makes a good impression on people, leading them to feel they are her friends. I will never forget how a native Skraeling woman at Straumsfjord sought out Gudrid, even though she could not communicate in our language. Somehow she had the impression that Gudrid would be safe to approach. Reasonable. Unlike me. That Skraeling made the right choice.

Frustrated, I mention Thorfinn Karlsefni's name, and this time the stout man nods vigorously. He explains how to get to the farm, although he cautions me that we will need horses. He recommends a nearby stable, then offers to store my trunks until I can return for them, provided I pay a rather large fee. He seems to assume I am wealthy, which is laughable, given the state of my weather-worn clothing. He must have seen our ship.

My crew relaxes in the cool of the inn. I pull Thorgrim aside to give him instructions.

Before I can even speak, he frowns. "I do not like to leave you alone."

He is so earnest and wistful, I wonder if he finds me attractive. It is unusual for men to do so, since they generally regard me first as a warrior, not a woman. But perhaps he has seen something he likes and feels emboldened now Ref is not with me.

I have no time for men.

I adjust Amoda in her sling. The child seems to have gained weight on the trip and I cannot wait to let her play and run. "Thorgrim, I will be traveling with the women and Atli to Thorfinn's farm, and we were told it is a long trek. You must stay here and sell the Icelandic ship." I hold up my hand to stay his protests. "You will keep the profits—you and the men. It will be your payment for accompanying me here. Of course, you will each have to secure your own return to Greenland."

It is self-serving to have Thorgrim sell the ship for me. But this way I am not connected with it, should the families of the dead come looking.

After realizing complaints are futile, he agrees to find a buyer for the ship. I take my leave of him, stalking around the small town for the stable. I finally find the dirty building by following the low neighs and snorts of the horses. It is built right onto the side of a small longhouse.

Once I settle our payment, the owner saddles worn-looking horses that aren't good for breeding, let alone riding. But at least they won't be too frisky for my old women. Bidding the crew farewell, we set off. Thorgrim shoots me a forlorn look, but I ignore it.

When the sun is high and the heat blistering, we finally discover the worn trail that leads toward Thorfinn's farm. Again, I find myself wondering why Gudrid is not yet known here. She was born in another part of Iceland, so perhaps these townspeople do not recognize her family name, even though her father was a chieftain.

As we pick our way to the top of a stone-strewn hill, the farm comes into view. It sits tucked into a green valley, and its size is impressive. We draw closer and I recognize Thorfinn himself, working on a tall sod and stone wall that encloses the animals, longhouse, and buildings. The wall is nearly as tall as his shoulder, and thick, as well. I cannot imagine the hours of labor required to maintain such a wall. Brattahlid only has low stone walls, and Leif's slaves maintain them.

"Thorfinn!" I shout, throwing one arm into the air. "How are you?"

"Freydis?" He drops his pick and walks up to my weary horse, taking the reins. His face and tunic are covered in sweat, but he is still one of the most striking men I have ever laid eyes on. "What has brought you all the way to Iceland? And how did you get here?"

His eyes sweep over us, taking our measure. What a sight we must be. The old hags pant as if they have walked the entire distance. Amoda launches into tired, short screeches that ring in my ears. Only Atli sits unperturbed on his mare, which has a sway-back drooping nearly to the ground.

I sigh. "There is much to explain, but I would like to tell the story only once, to you and to Gudrid. Perhaps we could go inside for a drink? And these animals need to be watered and stabled."

Thorfinn responds quickly. "Of course you are welcome. Come into the longhouse. My mother will have the slaves prepare a meal." His lips twitch downward. "But I am afraid Gudrid and the boys are not here."

"Where are they?"

"Living in a house by the coast."

He could not have shocked me more if he had pulled a sword and run my horse through. I sit stunned, ignoring Amoda's impassioned cries. So I am not the only woman in our family who is no longer with her husband.

THIRTY-THREE

IN THE COOL OF Thorfinn's longhouse, which is even longer than my father's oversized house at Brattahlid, we sip at our ale. From the elaborately carved, burly-wood beams of the house to the exotic foreign rugs on the stone floor, everything speaks to a level of established wealth my brother could only dream of attaining. Thorfinn Karlsefni has indeed reaped the rewards of his voyage to Straumsfjord and Vinland, but he is a trader who knows how to sell and barter goods to his advantage.

Thorfinn introduces his mother, Runa. Her white hair is so tightly tucked into a knot, it makes her eyes slant. She instructs her slaves to bring out dishes of cheese, bread, and dried berries. Given her sour-lipped glances and the irritated quirk of her brow, I suspect her hair isn't the only thing pulled tight. She is not happy her son brought us inside.

Oblivious to any unstated disapproval, Amoda runs in circles on the red rug, following the patterns beneath her feet. Thorfinn laughs as she begins tossing her copper curls about like a bucking horse.

"That girl shows no signs of stopping, Freydis. So like her mother. And where is that quiet father of hers?"

He levels his inscrutable cobalt blue gaze on me. I can never read this man, nor can I manipulate him. Every time I try to banter with him, it is like he sees past my light words, directly into my soul.

I don't know how Gudrid can stand it, but then again, she's practically perfect. She has nothing to hide.

I suppose being completely honest might put him at ease, and bluntness has always come easily to me.

"Ref and I are not together. He has stayed behind with his volva wench."

It takes a moment for my words to sink in. "Ref has another woman?" Thorfinn's gold-brown eyebrows arch in disbelief.

I make no attempt to explain Ref's dalliance with Kitta. Uncomfortable silence blankets the room, save the rhythmic, light slaps of Amoda's shoes on the rug. Finally, my people begin to shift around.

Atli slumps into his tall-backed wooden seat, placing his empty cup on the table. His heavy eyelids flutter closed. Dagmar and Huld politely pick up Amoda, taking her back to the cooking area, presumably to feed her.

Thorfinn's mother makes an attempt at conversation. "So you are Eirik the Red's daughter? We have heard of his exploits here in Iceland."

She emphasizes *exploits,* and it is clear she would love to inject a far more derogatory term for my father's behavior. It is no secret that he was finally banished from Iceland due to hot-headed, murderous retaliations for perceived slights, but I will not apologize for him. After all, he has told me the stories behind those events, and it seems his vengeance was well-grounded in necessity.

I grin, pulling out my curved knife. After making a little show of running my finger along its blade, I use it to pick at an invisible piece of food in my teeth. Finally, I say, "I am proud to be his daughter."

Thorfinn gives a short shake of his head, making it clear I am not to frighten his mother.

Like me, Thorfinn Karlsefni keeps a near-constant check on anything that could turn into a threat. Also like me, he knows how to quickly dispose of any threat that happens to develop.

I sheathe my knife.

It is my turn to ask questions. "And why does Gudrid not live here?"

Runa stands and stalks from the room, not even offering an excuse. Her rudeness answers my question, even as Thorfinn struggles to do so.

"My mother...she felt our match was beneath me."

I snort. "Gudrid is no beggar. You know her father was a chieftain and when he died, she became ward of my family—the founding family of Greenland. Now she has married you, one of the wealthiest men in Iceland. Are you not the man of this house? Your mother has no say in the matter."

He looks stunned, as if I have smacked him. Perhaps no one speaks to him this way.

I continue. "I must speak with your wife. If she *is* still your wife?"

For a moment, he looks like he wants to toss me out the door. Then he offers a slow, completely disarming smile.

"She is. And she always will be, Freydis."

I nearly choke. He pretends I am interested in him! Beautiful as the man is, he is dangerous as a snake in the water. Even if he did divorce Gudrid for some reason, we would kill each other on our wedding night.

"How *encouraging* to see your loyalty," I mock.

He looks out the window, slight smile lingering as he becomes serious again. "She will come tonight. She comes every night, so I can see our children."

"And why aren't the children with you? I am sure the Skraeling boys would be of help on your farm."

He glares at me. "They are not Skraelings. They are our children now."

"But your mother does not recognize them as such—am I correct? Perhaps this has caused her to reject Gudrid?"

Thorfinn huffs and stands. "I have wasted too much time here. If you want answers, ask Gudrid. You will see her tonight." He stands and walks to Atli's side, nudging him from his sleep. "Perhaps you could earn your bread while you are here?"

He is not fatherly with Atli, like Ref is. I feel a flare of protectiveness for my young warrior, but he accepts Thorfinn's suggestion easily enough.

Atli stretches to his full height, and he is half a head taller than Thorfinn. I find myself hoping Thorfinn will be impressed by his strength. I am proud of Atli as if he were my own son.

As they walk out, I sit in the cool of the longhouse, unwilling to move. Amoda happily babbles with my women, letting me know she's been fed and is ready for her nap. I should join her and rest, but I am not sure where Thorfinn would have us sleep.

Runa returns, a stiff smile on her face. "Please follow me to your house. I am not sure how long you plan to stay, but you are welcome here." She braids her lies with truths.

I retrieve Amoda from the old women and follow Runa onto a pathway that winds toward a series of huts. How many of Thorfinn's men live here at his farm? Have they traveled elsewhere? Surely there are more than enough huts to house a small army.

She takes a key from her belt and unlocks the door of a mid-sized earthen hut. As my eyes adjust to the interior, I take in gold and silver vases and statues on ornately carved chests. There is a heavy bed frame and a wardrobe for clothing. Sleeping benches line the walls. Stepping into the central room, I peer into a small door that leads to a hearth. Shelves are stocked with kitchen pots and utensils.

"Shall I have my women stay with me?" I ask. We could easily bunk together in such a large house.

She looks affronted. "Of course not. We will have houses for them, as well as for your man."

Even Brattahlid's wealth pales in comparison to this farm. I suppose Runa is somewhat justified in her haughty attitude. But I find her superior airs amusing.

"This will do." I am equally smug.

She sniffs. "When Gudrid arrives, I will send her to you."

I cannot resist such an opening. "And will she be staying overnight? Or perhaps she will be tempted to stay even longer with her husband?"

Amoda stretches and yawns, then lets out a cry. In a surprisingly tender gesture, Runa reaches out and touches one of my daughter's springy curls. "She has much fire, this little one. Like you, I would imagine, and like your father." She turns and walks out, shutting the door behind her.

It is impossible to know if she meant her words as a compliment or an insult. I place Amoda on the large bed and stretch out beside her, staring at the white clouds drifting above the smoke hole. Even the clouds seem strange in Iceland. Should we settle here? Or will my heart always be pulled toward Greenland?

As a cool, moss-scented breeze blows through the window, I close my eyes, curling around Amoda on the soft blanket. Even with my daughter tucked into the hollow of my body, I miss our silent, stoic protector.

Ref.

THIRTY-FOUR

I WAKE TO AMODA'S giggling. Gudrid has deposited her youngest, Bjorn, next to Amoda on the bed, and they play with wooden toys. Bjorn already outstrips Amoda in girth, although my daughter, who is a month older, is taller.

When I shift on the bed, Gudrid turns to me, her hair a curtain of pale silk on her shoulders. Time has been kind to Gudrid, as if her beautiful features have been honed with wisdom. Thorfinn is a fool not to protect such a treasure.

"I am thankful you came to us here," she says. "You and your people are welcome to stay with me, although our longhouse is packed tight already."

I shove myself into a sitting position, trying to catch her downcast gaze. "It is a disgrace. Thorfinn has plenty of housing here on his farm, and he shoves you off to a small house in the village? What is the meaning of it?"

She strokes Bjorn's thatch of blond hair. "His mother does not approve of me."

"That is nonsense! She has no basis for such a view."

Gudrid's voice is calm, as always. "She does not. Yet the Holy Book says not to return evil with evil, but to overcome it with good. I am trying to do so by bringing her daily treats—berries, herbs, whatever I have—so she sees I care for her as I would my own mother."

I cannot imagine taking this approach. When someone wishes me ill, when they actively work against my good or the good of my family, it seems only reasonable they should expect retaliation. If I do not protect us, then who will?

Valdis' hateful face flashes into my mind. I see the head of Tyr's wife, Suka's blood spattered on the snow…a gag works its way up my throat.

Gudrid notices. She deposits first Bjorn, then Amoda on the sheepskin rug with their toys. She puts a hand to my forehead. "Are you ill, sister?"

"No." The word sounds harsh, incomplete. But I cannot explain more. I am not ready to.

Gudrid never recoils in the face of my anger. She seems to realize it is part of who I am. In the face of her goodness, I always wish I could be more. More forgiving. More understanding. More kind.

"Thorfinn says you are no longer with Ref. Have you divorced?" She seems unsurprised, which disappoints me somehow.

"I do not know. I gave him leave to do as he wishes. He wanted Kitta, not me."

She gives a short laugh.

I glare at her. "How is that amusing?"

"Because you have told yourself a lie, Freydis. I have never seen a man more devoted to his wife than Ref is to you. He does not want Kitta."

"He said she was soft."

Gudrid glances over me, and I become aware of my clenched jaw and my rigid posture. I feel my own angular hardness as others must see it. The wary, watchful hardness of a warrior.

"It is true, you do not seem soft," she says. "But I see that softness in your eyes as you watch over your daughter. I see it when we have to say our farewells. You love your family. It is not a weakness, as you might think. It is your strength."

There is a knock at the door. "Enter," Gudrid says.

Thorfinn stands in the sunlit doorway. "Atli is loading the cart with split wood. I hope you do not mind if he accompanies Gudrid and our boys back to her house."

I realize he is speaking to me, asking my permission to send Atli along. "It is a good idea. Perhaps he could return the horses to town, as well. Do you have any men to send with him?"

"Most of my men are on a trading expedition now, but I will send Magnus with him."

"Magnus, your blind Irish shepherd? I doubt he will be much help moving wood."

Gudrid frowns. "Do not underestimate Magnus."

I stand to stretch. "I suppose he was helpful on our return voyage to Greenland."

Thorfinn seems to take this as an approval. As I turn back to Gudrid, he surprises me by walking around the bed to his wife. Taking her head in his hands, he presses a light kiss to her forehead, then another slow, burning kiss to her lips.

I turn away.

They do not speak, but he strides back out. I force myself to look at her, although her face is flushed.

"What is the meaning of this? You love each other, yet you cannot be affectionate before his mother? It is a mockery. How long have you been living in separate houses?"

She twists at her hair. "It has been since we traded goods in Norway. What a journey that was, Freydis! We dined in homes you would not imagine! But do not worry. I have already weathered a winter here in the smaller longhouse."

"You say this as if it is something to be proud of! Instead, it only shows me the selfishness of Thorfinn. I swear to you, Gudrid, I will not let you be alone another winter."

Her face brightens. "Then you will stay on with me?"

I grab her shoulder, wishing I could shake sense into her. "No. I will go and talk to that witch and tell her you will be living here from now on. I am not restrained by your Christian hesitations."

"If only you would be, I would not fear for your soul as I do, sister. Have you any restraints at all?"

Amoda gives a sharp cry as Bjorn snatches her wooden horse. Their behavior reflects our discord.

Instead of taking the toy and returning it as I would, Gudrid waits. "Let us watch to see how they overcome this," she says. "They are nearly cousins, though not by blood."

I remember my proud brother Thorstein, and wonder again how he persuaded Gudrid to marry him. He died not long into their marriage of an illness, giving her no children. Yet Gudrid has always seemed like another of Eirik's daughters—how my father doted on her when she was his ward!

Bjorn sits still, his chubby legs sprawled open, toys piled in between. Amoda has no toys, but clearly she only wants one.

"*Hross.*" She plaintively says "horse".

Bjorn pulls the simple toy up to examine it. He touches the smooth wood. Then, in a swift movement, he throws it into Amoda's lap.

My daughter's lips purse into a grin and she begins to push the horse along the rug, satisfied.

Gudrid's happy gaze meets mine. "You see, sometimes things resolve themselves. We do not have to intervene every time."

I hold my tongue, unwilling to agree. There have been so many events in my life when someone should have intervened and they did not. When I had no one to turn to, no one to protect me.

I swoop down to pick up Amoda and her horse. Bjorn's gray eyes, so like his father's, goggle up at me. Gudrid's green eyes do the same.

"All the same," I say finally, "when resolution is slow in coming, I will take action. I cannot do otherwise."

THIRTY-FIVE

CLAMBERING OVER THE ROUNDED, black-rocked hill, I wish I had not chosen this day to visit Gudrid in her village by the sea. The sun is high, the air is humid, and I forgot to bring a deerskin water bottle for the journey.

"Slow down, Atli." At my command, he slows so I can see the back of his blond hair. He has kept a pace I cannot possibly match.

There must be an easier path to Gudrid's house, perhaps around the hill, but it would have added a couple of hours to this already-wearying venture.

We pass ripening bilberries, and I stoop and pick a handful. The harvest is coming in and it will not be long until chilling winds begin to blow. I find it hard to believe that Runa has allowed us to stay so long, but she probably obeys her son's orders, and Thorfinn has benefited greatly from Atli's manpower about the farm. While Hol and Hellir do try to aid him, they are not yet fully-grown and their strength cannot match Atli's.

Amoda is almost too large to fit in the sling, and her legs slam into my thighs with each step. By the time I catch a glimpse of the village, my legs feel so battered, I am unsure how I will make the return journey today.

As we approach Gudrid's house, a large white dog careens toward us, its teeth bared and a growl deep in its throat. I stop short, wrapping my fingers tightly around my knife handle. Atli shoots me a questioning look, but I shake my head. If this animal is a problem, I can kill it much faster than he could.

Gudrid steps from her door and utters one sharp word, at which the irritating animal turns from us and trots to her side, dropping at her heel.

"I apologize. Frosty is not good with strangers."

I try not to scoff at the ridiculous name she has given her dog. "You still have a way with beasts." My voice carries more than a little reprimand for such a rude welcome.

She looks to the dog, her eyes wistful. "She is not the same as my wolf in Straumsfjord. But she would protect my children with her life and she keeps me company during my long days."

"It is good you have this protection," I acknowledge, giving her a small smile. As she turns to go inside, I give the dog a warning glare.

Gudrid's longhouse is small, yet quaint. She has transplanted low, flowering shrubs along the front of it. Although the turf walls and roof are overgrown with age, the light wood door draws the eye with a darker inlaid cross design.

In her last visit to Thorfinn's farm, Gudrid invited me to come and see her at her home. I have wondered if she needed more secrecy than what my longhouse could afford. I have not caught anyone lurking outside during our visits, but perhaps Gudrid simply feels more comfortable in her own surroundings.

"Come in and drink." She smiles at Atli as she offers, letting him know he is welcome, too.

We duck into the cool darkness of the longhouse and Gudrid motions to Deirdre, who brings us water that is so cool, it was probably drawn from a town well. Deirdre makes a great show of scooping up a piece of berry pastry for each of us, then dumping it halfheartedly into bowls, as if she has better things to do with her time than to serve the likes of us.

I squint up my eyes and give her a pinched smile. "Thank you so *very* much, Deirdre."

Atli devours his pastry in about two bites, then gulps his water. "Many thanks. Is there work for me?"

Gudrid pats his hand, a carved silver band shining on her finger. "What a thoughtful boy. Actually, Hol and Hellir tend to shirk at their duties when it comes to raking the hay. I am sure if you visited them in the field out back, they would be more motivated to work." She winks, motioning to a three-pronged wooden rake hanging by the door.

Atli nods, grabs the rake, and charges out the door, anxious to be on a mission.

"He is a good boy," Gudrid says. "Strong."

Gudrid's young son, Snorri, walks to my side. He is lean and tall. His large green eyes are the mirror image of his mother's, yet his gold-brown curls reflect his father's coloring. Hesitantly, he reaches for my hand. "Freydis," he says.

I nod, surprised he remembers me.

He holds my hand, unwilling to let go. I feel a part of my heart go out to the boy who was born at Straumsfjord, who bears the name of a fearsome warrior now dead. I want to ask him if he knows who he was named for, if he understands that honor, but I cannot form the words. Gudrid watches him too, as if spellbound by her own child.

Deirdre interrupts the moment by bustling to my side, her arms outstretched. "The child," she says, pointing to Amoda.

While I'm not fond of Deirdre, I know there is no caregiver more observant.

"The dog?" I ask.

Gudrid points outside. "She's probably out in the fields with the boys. You can close the door if you wish."

Slipping Amoda's sweaty body from the sling, I hand her over to Deirdre. The Irishwoman takes my daughter into a side room where I can hear Bjorn's cheery babbles. I stand and close the heavy wood door, exchanging the extra air flow for safety and privacy.

"I have come, as you asked," I say.

Sipping at her water, Gudrid nods. "I wanted to tell you something I have heard."

I lean forward. "What?"

"One of the men who bought my goats had loose lips. When he was here, he mentioned he'd seen a new ship at the dock—one that was quickly and quietly sold to a chieftain in the next village. He said he recognized the prow of that ship, and he knew the Icelander who owned it. Was this the ship you came in, Freydis?"

"Yes," I say.

"I thought so. And yet this man will not stop questioning where the rightful Icelandic owner is. Helgi, I think it was."

"I understand."

"The man also insinuated that rumors have been flying about what happened to this Helgi when he sailed to Vinland. He had promised to return to his mother by winter, and yet he has not appeared."

"Indeed." I pull at a wayward curl.

"Stop saying these things, Freydis! I know you, and I know when you are hiding something. You returned with one Icelandic girl, but no sign of Helgi. You had the larger ship, which I doubt he gave you willingly, no matter what goods you had to barter. Speak with me plain: where are the other Icelanders?"

It is no use hiding it from her, or from Thorfinn, I suppose. If the Icelanders are beginning to wonder, I need to let my family and hosts know a storm could be brewing.

"They were killed," I say.

Her eyes widen and she arches a light eyebrow. "No."

"I had my reasons," I explain.

"Who was killed? Helgi? His men?"

"Everyone. The men and the women. Kitta is the only one who survived."

Gudrid jumps to her feet and walks to my side, placing her hands on my shoulders as if she could stop me from doing any further damage. "Say this is not true!"

"Why do you think I am here? Leif found out—using torture on my men, no less—and he banished me from Brattahlid."

She sits on the bench next to me, sighing. "You are lucky he did not do worse. But tell me of your reasons."

The door of my silence is unlocked with Gudrid's earnest

request. I want to explain myself to someone since Tyr is the only one who knows the entire truth, and he will never leave the new lands.

I tell her of the volva, their cannibalism, their hatred of Skraelings, and their determination to take over Brattahlid. I share of Suka's death, of Valdis' evil intent toward Atli, and of her plan to steal my baby when it was born. I also tell how she forced Kitta to use her body for personal gain. Finally, I explain how the volva died.

When I finish speaking, Gudrid's eyes hold mine, as if she is searching for any hint of a lie. When she does not find one, she wraps her arms around me.

"You have been holding this inside, all these months? What is Ref's part in this?"

"He merely followed my commands. I...convinced him the Icelanders had hurt me."

"And you murdered the women yourself?"

"I had to. I could not let the men do it."

"And Kitta knows of this?"

"She does, but she is indebted to me for sparing her life. Twice, actually. I did not kill her with the Icelanders and I did not kill her when I found her in my own bed with my husband."

Waves of memories wash over me—the vivid red of Valdis' blood on her white hair. Kitta's pale exposed legs. My husband, exulting when Amoda was born on the ship. I lean forward and press my fingers into my temples, wishing I could rub out the blood and anger that seem to stain my life.

Gudrid does not touch me, does not speak. Will she console me? Will she hate me? Somehow, the only thing that matters is if this

Christian woman can forgive my heinous sins. I do not deserve her forgiveness. I have blotted the family name and I have likely made us all vulnerable to Icelandic retribution.

"I am not the one to offer forgiveness," she says, as if she has read my tortured thoughts. She places a hand on my curls, smoothing them down my back. "Nor does it matter what Leif supposes, or even Finn, for that matter. You are mired in blood guilt, and it will eat you alive if you do not confess it."

"To the Icelanders' families?"

"No. They cannot understand what depths that rogue volva stooped to—indeed, she would have been killed by her own kind, had she stayed here. The volva do not allow cannibalism. Doubtless, Valdis sailed to the new lands with the intent of setting up her own religion, where she would not be under anyone's thumb."

I peer up into Gudrid's soft eyes. "Then who shall I confess to? I have told you already. My husband...he no longer cares what I have done or will do."

"To God." She says this as if it is the most obvious thing in the world.

"Which god? I hold loyalty to none. They will not hear me."

"There is only one God, Freydis. What's more, I believe you know this is true and that you've been trying to escape Him for years. You must have seen His hand—even at Straumsfjord. I remember when you stood there and fought the Skraelings for us. You were not killed."

"My babe was stillborn that day. I might as well have been killed."

"The babe was dead long before that fight," she says, her voice soothing. "I suspected it, but held out hope I was mistaken."

"If your god is good, why did he take my firstborn son at all?"

"I do not know, but will you spend your life raging against a power you can never fight? God let you live for a reason. Perhaps that reason was to give birth to your daughter. Perhaps that reason was to protect your family from a threat we could not have suspected or prepared for. Perhaps that reason was to live to see this day, the day you realized you have done wrong and need forgiveness. I do not know, but don't let this day slide into another without asking the only God for His forgiveness, sister."

"Why should he care for me?"

"Because He created you."

"He created a forest child." I laugh sharply.

"Of course He did. He knew you would grow up like your father, a fearsome warrior and a skilled sailor—one unafraid to sail to unexplored lands. He also knew you would protect those you loved, time and time again, never asking for thanks or praise. You are not perfect, Freydis, but no one is. With the forgiveness and help of the one true God, you will begin to see new opportunities."

Opportunities. I thought those had died along with my reputation at Brattahlid, or with the death of my marriage.

Amoda's whining interrupts my thoughts, and Deirdre pokes her head around the doorframe. "I believe your daughter wishes for you."

Gudrid grabs my hand. "Do not forget these things."

I smile. I will not forget. And I will not delay. I rush to the door, throwing it open and charging out. I look up at the cloudless pale sky, shimmering with heat.

"Forgive me, God! I am a murderer, and I have done many wrongs."

Gudrid follows me and links her arm with mine. In a low voice, she asks, "Do you believe in the Christ who has died on the cross for your sins?"

"Yes!"

"Are you willing to serve Him all your days? And not your own selfish desires?"

"I want to, but it will be difficult."

Gudrid laughs, and it sounds like water trickling into my desert of loneliness. Deirdre emerges from the front door with Amoda in her arms, a questioning look on her face.

"You must tell God these things and always be honest with Him," Gudrid says. "He loves you more than anyone on earth ever can. He already knows the things you have told no one about. He wants to comfort you."

A flood of emotion wells in my chest. Happiness, not contingent on anything around me. Peace with who I am. Thankfulness for a forgiveness I could not earn.

As I take Amoda into my arms and swing her in a circle, a final emotion nearly cripples me. Regret. I regret that I have left my husband, who loves his daughter as much as I do. I took her from him, with the intent that he never see her again.

Amoda pats at my cheek, and only then do I realize that my face is wet with tears.

THIRTY-SIX

AS THE HARVEST RIPENS, Runa and I ease into a companionable silence. She hugs Amoda and murmurs to her when we visit her longhouse, and I refrain from any cutting remarks. We go about our tasks alone, neither of us asking for help.

I know God helps me keep my silence when Gudrid pays us visits. Every time she catches Thorfinn's eyes, I can feel the heat between them. It is not right for a woman so in love with her husband to be separated from him, simply because of her mother-in-law's command.

Or for any other reason.

I have too much time for reflection here. Even as I rehearse Ref's sins, I believe some part of me has started to fall in love with my husband. If I am honest, I married Ref because I wanted to possess someone from a good family, someone who had the wealth I did not.

And when I was nearly able to buy the farm, what happened? My dreams faded before my eyes. Even my husband abandoned me and threw me on the negligible mercy of my brother.

Yet why should this surprise me? My spirit resonates with the truth that for most of our marriage, I have offered Ref nothing but disdain.

Memories rise up like living beings when I am alone, surrounding and taunting me. It is not hard to imagine Ref's wide hands stroking my arms. I can easily taste the salt from his lips. And when I remember his entrancing eyes and how they hardly left my face, I can hardly breathe. Love has struck me harder now than it ever did before we married.

I try to stoke the fire of hatred for Kitta, but if I am honest, I know she was easily led astray. She was alone in a new land, unsure who to side with. Thanks to Valdis, Kitta had learned that her body was nothing more than a bargaining tool, a way to ensure she was looked after.

She was weak. Ref was weak.

But now I am weak.

Shaking these thoughts aside, I strap on my knife sheath. There is a fresh bite in the air that seems to prod me from our cozy longhouse. By the fire, Dagmar repairs a hole in one of my leather shoes, dropping lazy stitches into it. Amoda sucks on her thumb as she sleeps nearby.

"I am going to check my traps," I say. "Maybe I will gather berries."

"Do not stay too long," Dagmar warns. "That woman said we are invited to the evening meal since Gudrid will be here."

I grin. Aware of my initial dislike for Runa, Dagmar always refers to her as "that woman."

"I will return before then. We've only just finished the mid-day meal, Dagmar."

The old woman shushes me, ignoring my impertinence and returning to her slow needlework.

The landscape seems to roll out before me, from the cornflower-blue skies to the waterfalls tumbling over the distant mountains. The grass is partially harvested, and the men have propped it in neat stacks against the wall so it can thoroughly dry. Later, they will move the hay, covering it with turf for the winter.

Will we be staying in Thorfinn's longhouse this winter? Atli and my old women seem to enjoy their peaceful lives in Iceland. Amoda loves seeing her many cousins and being doted on. I have independence here, coming and going as I please. I can think of no reason to leave.

I spot several ripe blueberries and stoop to pick them, but realize I forgot to bring a pouch or a basket for my finds. A lingering, nameless distraction has made me forget the things I should not.

Although I do not take my usual pains to walk quietly and listen for animal movements, I have no cause to fear. Iceland harbors no human predators, such as Greenland's white bears and wolves. So far, my traps have only caught mink and rabbits. I have seen a fox, but it hardly seemed aggressive. Gudrid's protective dog seems like the most fearsome animal I'm apt to encounter here.

I pop blueberries into my mouth, savoring their sweetness. An echoing shout sounds behind me, and I turn.

Atli runs toward me, easily overtaking my slow pace. "Checking traps?"

I nod. "And what are you doing this fine day? Does Thorfinn have you harvesting?"

"Barley," he says.

We walk past one of Thorfinn's summer pastures. Plump cattle munch on the thick grasses. The milk cows are closer to the longhouse so they can be milked daily. Runa's slaves use the milk to make some of the richest *skyr* I have ever tasted, and it is even better mixed with Gudrid's bilberry jam.

"They are healthy animals," Atli says. "Thorfinn is careful with his breeding. The bulls are not so hostile as others I have seen."

I remember Gudrid's raging bull and how it tried to attack her at Straumsfjord. I managed to distract it and sink an arrow into its side, but the stupid beast did not die. It was actually a good thing it survived, since it later gored several Skraelings who attacked our camp.

"You like living here?" I ask.

He gives me a long look, trying to understand why I ask. "Yes. Although my heart still cries out for Norway sometimes, Iceland pleases me. And Thorfinn has taught me much."

I am thankful for Thorfinn. His sometimes-gruff exterior hides a giving heart. I have offered him payment for our stay here, but he will not accept it. He claims that Atli's help on the farm is payment enough. The man works harder than anyone I have ever known, but I suspect he is trying to distract himself from his wife's absence.

I do not think Thorfinn and Gudrid have kept themselves physically separate, however. We pretend not to notice when they disappear into empty houses on her visits here.

I shake my head, willing my thoughts away from such a perilous subject.

Atli misunderstands my gesture. His voice is laced with sudden doubt. "You do not want to stay here?"

I pat his strong arm. "I find it very suitable, although I miss hunting with my bow."

His blue eyes pierce my own. "Perhaps you are missing Ref."

I drop my gaze, looking for berries again. I do not have the heart to address his impertinence.

"I miss him, too," he continues. "He taught me many things. I had only just begun to learn to carve—"

"We will not speak of him." I hand him several blueberries to keep his mouth busy.

As we top a small hill, I turn to survey the farmland. A slim, dark boy zigzags toward us. Hellir is not loud by nature, but he shouts at us boldly.

"Come now! Riders are nearly upon the farm!"

THIRTY-SEVEN

WE RUN TOWARD THE longhouse. Hellir has precious little information to share. He only says that Thorfinn sent him and that there are about six people on horses. It hardly sounds like a war party, but as the house comes into view over the final rise, we unsheathe our knives and creep toward the back fence.

I can make out Thorfinn's back; his curly hair is pulled back in a leather tie. He is making wide arm gestures, but it's impossible to determine if they are hostile or simply enthusiastic.

"I can go," Atli offers.

I thrust my arm lengthwise across his chest, as if shielding him from an invisible blow. "Absolutely not."

Hellir has flattened his body on the ground. He is too young to fight and wise enough to realize I won't let him try.

I pray Gudrid is not traveling here now, bringing her younger children along to meet their brothers.

A sword hilt glints in the sunlight as one of the horses turn sideways. Will these riders dismount? Or are they demanding something from Thorfinn, ready to charge and fight if he does not comply?

Perhaps the Icelandic families have come for me. If Leif did not guard his lips, the story of our massacre will have spread. Or maybe the man who recognized Helgi's ship has continued his prying and hit upon the truth.

It is obvious what I have to do.

I stand, even as Atli pulls on my skirt hem, nearly tripping me. I kick loose of him, determined to protect these boys who have many years left in their lives.

The riders' faces become clearer as I stride closer. One is a woman. A dark-haired woman who looks remarkably like Kitta.

As she lifts her pale face, turning from Thorfinn to me, I gasp.

It *is* Kitta.

And seated next to her on a borrowed Icelandic horse is my husband.

"Freydis." Ref's voice ripples into the silence that has fallen.

My feet seem to have frozen in place, and I cannot move.

Thorfinn turns and smiles. "Look who has come to see you, Freydis! He has not forgotten you after all."

I know Thorfinn is merely teasing me, but he does not understand the entire story. He does not know that my husband boldly flaunts his little woman, sailing with her all the way to the northern shore of Iceland...why? To tell me he has married her? To rub my face in his betrayal?

Thorfinn moves on to speak to another rider. It seems Ref has brought his own little crew along, as I did when we came here.

"You have a ship?" I can't hold back from asking.

"I built one," Ref says simply.

"A knarr?"

"A smaller longship. I was not transporting animals or plundering Iceland on this particular voyage." His lips turn up into a grin.

I am in no mood for sport. I jerk my thumb toward Kitta, who has wisely fixed her eyes on the ground in front of her.

"And you have brought her? Did you expect me to welcome both of you with my arms open? Did you not guess I would send you both away as soon as I saw you?"

Ref swings his legs over the saddle and walks toward me. Although he's not a tall man, his frame is well-fitted together and has the rough-hewn muscles of a workman.

I stand on a little rise, so I look down at him as he approaches. Perhaps I have always visualized Ref standing beneath me. It makes it easier to give commands.

But he does not stop walking until he stands above me. I wait for an explanation of Kitta's presence, but he offers none.

His unusual eyes slowly explore my own, and I feel as if all my emotions are laid bare. Longing. Anguish. Hatred.

And finally, he sees what I try to hide. Love.

He makes a low noise, deep in his throat. His hand slides under my hair, gently pulling my neck forward. His lips have covered mine before I can even step back.

As his kiss warms me, I do not want to step away. I let my fingers fold into the thick hair on top of his head. His kiss is full of regret, yet charged with longing and determination unlike anything I have felt from him before.

This much I know: he does not love Kitta. My husband has never stopped loving me.

～

Runa rushes out, greeting everyone like they are a delegation come to call on royalty. She sets her slaves to work on the evening meal.

Ref and I fall into a surprisingly easy, silent communion. I motion for Atli and Hellir to approach. Atli extends an arm and clasps Ref's, giving him the serious look of a man who has been playing the protector. Appreciation shines in Ref's eyes as he praises Atli for helping us settle at the farm.

Dagmar emerges from our longhouse to see what the clamor is. Amoda rubs at her eyes, trying to blink off the sunlight.

Ref reaches her side in just a few strides, taking her into his arms and hugging her tightly. "My sweet girl," he murmurs over and over into her red curls.

Runa seems to make the connection. She turns to me. "This is your man? But I thought—"

"He never divorced me," I say.

The older woman's eyes widen. Maybe she's incredulous anyone would want to stay married to me. I cannot hold back my smile as I tell her what I have just admitted to myself.

"He loves me."

Hearing my words, Kitta dismounts and stumbles toward the longhouse. A ridiculous kindness propels me forward.

I take her arm and it softens in my grip as if her bones have turned to water. "He brought you home, didn't he?"

Tear-filled eyes meet mine. "Yes, m'lady."

"Your parents...will they take you back?"

"I do not know for certain, but I believe they will be glad for me to aid the villagers with their births. Perhaps I will even be paid for it."

"You will not become a volva."

She nods. "Never."

"Then you must stay here until we can take you home. I forgive you." The words spring from my mouth unbidden, but I find them surprisingly true. I have experienced great forgiveness. There is no reason I should not extend it to this misguided, homeless girl.

THIRTY-EIGHT

IF I CLOSED MY eyes, it would seem we were back at Brattahlid, so joyous is our feasting tonight.

Gudrid has arrived, eagerly listening to Hellir as he recounts his adventures of the day. Her boy feels like a big man, even though he would have run like anyone else his age, should the riders have turned out to be hostile.

Bjorn wriggles in his seat, then launches into a series of short screeches. Concerned, Gudrid leans toward him, but he is grasping for Amoda, who sits on my lap. My girl is already stuffed with food, and she claps in Bjorn's direction, eager to play. I motion toward Dagmar, but Ref jumps from his seat near Thorfinn.

"I will take the children."

It is unusual for a man to leave his conversation with other men to watch over children. In the past, I might have scoffed at this gesture, but now I realize it is one of my husband's strengths. Just as my father delighted in my presence, now Ref delights in Amoda's.

Heat suffuses my cheeks as Ref looks up from the children. My husband also delights in me.

Gudrid does not miss a thing. "You are reconciled! How wonderful! God has changed your heart."

Although we certainly have not reconciled yet, I do not correct Gudrid. I know she is longing for her own resolution with her husband, which seems impossible with Runa's ungrounded misgivings. I lean on the table, accidently grinding my elbow into my cabbage.

"You must talk with Runa. She must have noticed how helpful you are, how much her son adores you."

"Sometimes that is not enough," she says shortly.

"That is ridiculous," I say, spearing my meat with my fork. "How many times must we have this conversation before you do something about it?"

"My way is not your way, Freydis."

"Well, sometimes my way is right."

She grins. "I have to ask myself what God would have me to do."

"Why wouldn't He want you to take a stand? Runa is in the wrong here."

Thorfinn's mother glances down at me from her place near the head of the long table, as if she realizes I am plotting against her.

I lower my voice a notch. "I think she would be reasonable if you simply *approached* her about this. It is awkward for everyone."

Gudrid's eyebrows shoot upward, her green eyes gleaming in the firelight. "It is?"

I snort. "Haven't you noticed how we tiptoe around the two of you? You are in a world of your own as it is. It only makes things difficult for the rest of us—your boys included. They could be working together, learning from their father, instead of traveling back and forth like strangers."

"The wounds of a friend are faithful," she intones.

"What is that?"

"Words from the Holy Book. Your tongue has always lashed like a whip, but now that you have converted, I see that God is using your words to challenge me. I will approach Runa. You are right, I am making our family weak because I have refused to act."

I smile, victorious.

She nudges me in the ribs with her elbow. "Don't gloat too much, sister. Pride might go before a fall—more words from the Holy Book."

Glancing over at Ref, a shiver moves up my spine. "I've fallen as far as I ever want to, striving for a better position."

Gudrid beams at me, and I can feel Thorfinn staring at her across the table. She catches his eye and grows serious once again. "I have fallen too," she says, her voice low. "I forgot who I was. I am the wife of Thorfinn Karlsefni, leader of a successful expedition to Vinland. I am the mother of his children. My place is at his side, no matter where we move. I will not cower in fear."

Runa watches us closely, as well she should. Our agreement has become something powerful, and it can only grow more powerful as we ask the one true God to aid us. Women can cause the deepest rifts, but they can also bind the deepest wounds.

Although it is late when Finn accompanies Gudrid back to her home, the daylight does not fade early this time of year. Tonight, as fluffy charcoal clouds squat low in the pale pink skies, Atli suggests building a fire outside.

Dagmar groans of the hour, standing slowly. "I am not as spry as I once was, m'lady."

I cannot picture Dagmar ever feeling spry. "Of course. You wish to go to your hut?"

She nods and walks toward the doorway, glancing at Ref on her way. He sits at the table, crooning to Amoda in a low voice and gently bouncing her on his lap. She rubs at her long lashes with her fists, her pink mouth shaping into an extended yawn.

Realizing Dagmar is lingering so she can put Amoda to bed for me, I reluctantly leave the soft warmth of the sheepskin-covered bench I have been sitting on. I reach for Amoda, and although she can barely keep her eyes open, she whines to stay with her father. He plants kisses all over her fair face, then gives her to me.

I take her to Dagmar and give instructions. "Be sure to wash her well. She sleeps better when she is clean."

Dagmar nods and allows me a final goodnight kiss before whisking Amoda out the door.

Ref stands and stretches. His short tunic slides up, revealing the lean muscles of his stomach. He has not been eating enough.

Atli gives a short whistle. As if responding to an unspoken request, Ref picks up two chairs and carries them outside. I do the same, and in a short time we have several grouped around the bonfire. Ref's sailors join us, as well as Runa and Kitta. At least there is plenty of housing for all of us, but I do wonder where Ref will sleep.

Falling into a discussion with the sailors, Atli embellishes the tale of our voyage here, making it sound far more dangerous than it actually was. Runa and Kitta lean toward each other, sharing stories of old families in Iceland. Their laughter rises above the murmur of the sailors' voices.

I speak to no one, but I am not uncomfortable. There is a solace here in Iceland that I have not found in all my travels, a promise that a new life could be mine. My heart feels as if it has been swept clean.

As a smile plays about my lips, I feel someone staring. Angling my chair closer to the fire, I catch Ref's eyes on me, lit by the fire's glow.

"Our voyage was slow without you," he says. "You are far better at catching the wind and making short work of a long journey."

I take up a stick and poke at the fire. He knows I am not ready to thank him for his praise.

He continues. "Thorfinn has offered us housing until we are ready to leave. Kitta is anxious to go home. It will be quite a journey to her family. Perhaps my men can stay behind to help with the farm work."

"Or I could take her home for you." My words are meant to be kind, but they come out sounding pinched. "She does not know how to fight, should she run into trouble."

He nods thoughtfully. "She cannot protect herself, as you can."

I shift in my chair, uncomfortable with the awe in his tone. Thankfully, Atli asks Ref a question about the trees in Iceland, allowing me to sink once again into my own musings.

One stubborn idea thrusts itself to the forefront: we could be happy here in Iceland. We could be a family once again.

THIRTY-NINE

RETURNING TO MY LONGHOUSE as the sky finally darkens, I take up a small oil lamp, a clean shift, and a large square of fleece. Dagmar rouses and agrees to sit with my sleeping daughter until I return from the farm bath-house that is built over a hot spring. Although it is a long trudge out to the edge of the enclosed land, the warm water will take the chill from my bones and give me the opportunity to pray with no distractions.

I duck through the low, water-warped doorway, breathing in the slightly mildewed smell. I place my lamp in a dry crevice near the wall, where it casts shadows over the tiny room. Staying in a hunched position, I strip and pile my clothing on the stone floor near the fleece. Using my toes and the flickering light, I feel my way along the slippery rocks to an edge where I can sit, then I slip into the milky blue-white water. I dunk my head in it, reveling in its comforting warmth.

Runa has left one of her lavender soaps nearby, so I take it to scrub my body and hair. The soap rinses off easily, and I use my fingers to pull the snarls from my wet curls. I wish Runa would have left a comb behind, as well.

I pray aloud, asking God for wisdom as a mother and even as a wife. All my questions about Ref seem irreverent, and drowsiness has come on the heels of my cleanliness. I prop my elbows on the ledge, ready to jump out.

But the door scrapes and begins to edge open. I stare at the wooden board sitting useless on the inside of the door. I forgot to push it into a locked position.

I have no knife. The moment someone steps in, the lamp will indicate that someone is in here.

If I stand, I have nowhere to hide, so I will give myself a momentary advantage. Taking a deep breath, I sink into the water.

Footsteps pound and then someone stops, examining the pile of clothing on the floor. I was a fool to leave my knife on my belt instead of positioning it nearby. A man's muffled voice breaks the silence. Prising my fingers between rocks, I force myself lower.

Suddenly, hands plunge into the water and grab my arms. I writhe like a thrashing eel, but I cannot fight him off. I am pulled up until the dimming light hits my head and torso.

Defiant, I raise my eyes to meet my captor.

Ref squats next to the water, keeping me firmly in his grip. His eyes play over my body. "It was not wise to come here alone. Where is your knife?"

Still short of breath, I sputter my answer. "Do not assume I am without it. You are lucky I did not kill you straightaway."

He smiles, releasing my arms. "Perhaps I am."

"Were you following me?"

He does not answer directly. "Thorfinn mentioned the bathhouse and I wanted to clean myself from our journey."

"I was just getting out," I say. "I will leave you alone."

His brow crinkles. "Please don't."

Standing in the water, I turn my back to him. "I need to get back to Amoda."

He leans forward, running his fingertips firmly along my shoulder blades, as if I am a piece of wood he is smoothing. His palm widens, fingers protectively clamping on my shoulder.

"Stay," he commands.

I defy his forceful request by pulling up on the other side of the water hole, but he slips in behind me with barely a splash. His arms circle my waist and he moves closer, his tunic floating up behind me. He must still be fully dressed.

"My hair needs to be washed." His low voice is charged.

More than anything, Ref loves to have his head rubbed. I turn and face him. I take in his gray-flecked hair, so thick on the top. My gaze slides to first his blue eye, then his green, then on to his lips.

Perhaps Kitta has washed his hair, rubbed his head. She has kissed those lips.

"No. She has been with you."

He lowers his eyes, then meets mine again, earnest. "Once."

Ref would not lie to me. It was only one time.

I try not to soften, but my voice betrays me, coming out as a wounded whisper. "I was not enough for you."

He slowly extends his hand, fingering one of my curls as carefully as if it were glass. "No, Freydis. You were too much for me. I have never known a woman like you, nor has anyone else. I cannot handle you, I cannot stop you, and I do not know how to love you."

His words unlock something inside of me. I take his face in both my hands.

"Like this," I say, and kiss him.

When we finally leave the bath-house, I am quite sure Dagmar has fallen asleep, most likely on my bed.

"Where will you sleep?" I ask.

"Wherever you sleep." He pats my backside.

I don't refuse him. As we top a slight rise, the main longhouse comes into view. I stop, taking a closer look. Flames leap from the turf roof of the longhouse, lighting it as bright as day.

I thrust my hand out, keeping my voice low. "Knife."

Ref hands me my knife belt as he yanks his shoes on. "Why?"

"That is no normal fire. Do you see the men on horseback? The longhouse is surrounded. Go rouse Atli and your men."

"You will protect Amoda?" he asks, grabbing for my arm as he stumbles over a branch.

"Yes. You gather the men and weapons and I will see you at the longhouse, as soon as she is safe."

As I reach my longhouse door, I have my key and knife ready. I unlock the door and burst in, startling Dagmar from her comfortable position on the foot of my bed.

"Get up, woman! Enemies are upon us!"

She finds the baby sling and straps it over herself, then jostles Amoda's sleeping body into it. I take my sword and shield from the wall.

Amoda nods to one side, startling herself awake. She whimpers in preparation for a full wail, but I step over and place a hand over her mouth, shaking my head.

"No, daughter. No crying now," I order.

Sensing my urgency, her eyes widen and fill with tears, but she falls silent. I might have just scared my baby half to death.

I turn to the old woman. "The sheepcote is not far—just over that side wall. Take her there, hide among the sheep, and wait for rescue."

I do not tell her to wait for me, because I might not return.

Dagmar lurches out the back door, and I run out the front, toward the flames. As I draw closer to the longhouse, it becomes clear that the cheering invaders believe they have killed everyone inside.

They came to murder, and even before their leader's white-blond hair catches the light, I know that the Icelanders have come for revenge.

As I draw my sword, Ref emerges from the darkness with Atli and a handful of men clustered behind him. He hesitates. "Should we attack them directly?"

A woman screams inside the longhouse, and the Icelandic leader stalks to the door. "Time to let the piglets out," he says. "Let's give them some fresh air."

He removes the pieces of wood they have used to block the door and shoves it open. Kitta stumbles out blindly, her face and clothing on fire. She rolls on the ground, smearing herself with dirt even as she screams in pain.

"We have a lively one." One of the men reaches down and jerks her upright. He flicks his fingers through her dark hair, ignoring her burned face. "It's not the redhead they told us about, but I think this one could be of use."

The blond man nods and rides over, yanking her onto his horse. Fire begins to engulf the walls, but no one else appears in the doorway.

"Freydis Eiriksdottir might be dead, but burn all the other houses to be sure," he says. "Meet me at the spot we agreed on when your task is done."

His men fan out on their horses to obey, torches held aloft so they can set the farm on fire. The leader trots down the path toward the village, Kitta bouncing on the side of the horse as if she's half-dead already.

"They cannot do this," I say.

Ref agrees. "Once we unseat them from the horses, they will be ours." He lifts, then drops his hand, and three of his men who carry spears run toward the horsemen. The others fall in behind with swords and axes. Ref restrains Atli by laying a hand on his arm—he wants to fight alongside the young warrior who is so like a son.

I know Ref cannot leave the farm until the Icelanders are routed. "I will take a horse and follow Kitta," I say.

He is surprised, but wisely says nothing against my plan. "Go. I will catch up to you as soon as I can."

I race toward the barn where Ref's borrowed horses are stabled. A larger stallion neighs at me and I swing onto him, hoping he will be anxious enough to move quickly.

The blazing longhouse lights the sky, so we find the path with little trouble. I determine to go as far as I can without a torch, although if the Icelander has stopped, he will hear our approaching hoofbeats.

I think of Kitta's blistered face, back, and arms. She will never be the same after this attack. And Thorfinn…if he did not escape, I cannot think of the anguish Gudrid will suffer. Once again, I have brought pain to everyone I get close to.

FORTY

MY STALLION POUNDS THROUGH the night's silence until the black hill looms ahead. Voices float toward me and I draw on the reins. Someone is tucked into the small woods nearby.

"My men will come soon and then we will see who can afford to buy you." I recognize the Icelandic leader's voice.

"My friends will not leave me alone." Kitta's reply sounds bold, but I know inside she quakes with fear. "Besides, I am an Icelander, like yourself. I was on my way to my own family."

"Makes no difference to me. You stayed with Thorfinn Karlsefni, who should have turned Eirik's daughter out on her heel. She has likely killed my own brother and only the gods know how many others."

There is no response. Kitta has chosen to hold her tongue about the extent of our massacre in Vinland.

A small fire sparks to life, illuminating the scene. Kitta sits on one side of the fire, the Icelander on the other. I hope this means he does not plan to take advantage of her.

The air has become colder and the chill easily penetrates my light linen shift. I run my fingers over the saddle, hoping someone might have left a cloak or blanket strapped to it.

My horse chooses this moment to give a loud, prolonged whinny.

The Icelander stands. I am in the middle of a field and there is nowhere to hide my stallion. I mount up anyway, steering the animal toward a low outcropping of rock we passed on the way here. The horse will be visible, but only if the Icelander takes up a torch to make a thorough search.

I offer feverish, silent prayers that God would hide my horse and shut its mouth, that Ref will have a quick victory and come to my aid soon, and that Thorfinn and everyone in the longhouse survived.

Just as silence has fallen once again, there is a distinct shout in the distance. It is Kitta.

"No!"

She sounds terrified. I cannot find a place to tether the horse, so I leave him munching on grass and creep closer to the trees. The Icelander stretches before the fire, but Kitta is tied up by her feet, dangling over the now-roaring flames.

He knows someone is here, and he is taunting me.

It seems unlikely I can make a covert approach, but I must try. I cannot leave the girl that way. Her face has been burned once tonight, and I cannot allow it to happen again, no matter what she did with my husband.

Torn between my curved knife and my sword, I finally decide on the knife. I am fastest with that, as long as I can get close to the man. And I have ways of getting close.

Kitta's continued screams work in my favor, cloaking my advance. I skirt the woods and during a particularly passionate wail, I scramble toward the tree closest to Kitta. With all the blood rushing to her head, she'll soon lose the energy to scream. I need to get to her before she falls silent and faints.

The tree is not ideal for climbing. Limbs are dying and one even cracks off below my foot, leaving me hanging by my hands for a moment. The Icelander still peers away from us, expecting to see the horse.

I reach a reasonably stable limb that overhangs Kitta. She does not look up, her weak body arching toward the ground.

Do I have the strength to cut her free and pull her up by the small loop of rope? I doubt it. If I could somehow get her attention, there is a chance that she could reach up to take my hands, but if her attempt failed, the Icelander would see me and have the advantage.

I've left myself no other choice. I must jump to the ground and slit his throat, just as I would a deer.

I grip my knife in one hand, shifting so that I will drop directly behind the large man below. It is a long fall, but I am fairly sure I can land on my feet.

Just as I prepare to launch from the limb, Kitta looks up and gasps. The Icelander's pale eyes whip toward me and he grins like a loosed demon. Pulling his sword, he stabs into the air at me.

I back up to avoid the blade's tip, but a terrible crack sounds and my limb snaps. I grasp blindly as I plummet onto the hard ground, my knife arm pinned beneath me. Using only my feet, I shove myself backward, but it takes only a heartbeat for the man to step astride my torso, pinning my shift to the ground with his boots.

Leaning down, he makes his face level with mine. His hot breath blasts me. He cannot hide his excitement. "I do believe I've caught more than I bargained for with this trap. I'm surprised you're so loyal to your useless friend, *Freydis Eiriksdottir*."

He grabs me and rolls me over, shooting fresh pain through my arm. I fear it is broken, it's so stiff. I cannot hold back my scream as he pulls both my wrists behind my back, securing them with a length of rope.

Kitta begins to cry, and the man is quickly frustrated with her. He reaches up and cuts her rope, barely catching her before her face is scorched by the blazing fire.

He dumps her on the ground like a sack of wheat. The rope on her hands hangs loosely, but he must believe she won't try to escape.

Returning to me, he ties my feet and drags me over to a tree. "I will admit that was a clever attempt. I should have known you would be crafty, given the fact that you were able to kill my brother. You *did* kill him, didn't you?"

I won't admit anything to this man. My lips tighten into a straight line.

He kicks at a rock. "It is wise that you don't speak, because I will not accept lies. My friend saw Helgi's ship in the harbor, but it was the strangest thing: there was no Helgi. My brother would not leave his ship, Freydis Eiriksdottir. And Finnbogi would not leave Helgi. The last I heard, they had thrown their lot in with you for their voyage to Vinland."

Coming closer, he snatches a handful of my shift, pulling me up to meet his eyes. "And a rumor from Greenland has reached my ears, that you were the one who brought Helgi's ship back, with no Icelanders aboard."

I've had enough. I spit in his face. It splatters his open mouth.

He smiles and slowly licks the spit off. "My, but you're fiery, aren't you?"

"My men will come looking for me," I say.

He purses his lips, thoughtful. "It is wise to be hopeful. But at some point you will see they are all dead and it is best to tell me what happened."

Kitta's cries have not stopped, but I can barely hear them anymore. Tears streak the soot on her face, showing the fire-reddened skin beneath. It would be best if she could fall asleep, but her fear and pain will not allow it.

Maybe I can get us out of this and appease him.

"I will tell everyone what happened—at a meeting of the Althing. I want my brother beside me."

Whether Leif would sail to Iceland to speak for me at their yearly gathering of lawgivers, I do not know. But I am sure this Icelander knows who my brother is.

He hesitates, considering. Then he gives me another smile. "Do you think you can scare me? I am not afraid of Leif Eiriksson. We all know your family left this island in disgrace because your father broke our laws. You will not be shown mercy here, even if your Christian brother sails over to speak for you."

I smile back, as if I have a deadly secret of my own. In reality, I wish I could cut my throbbing arm off and drift to sleep for a week.

The man seems to sense my pain. "I will say this: I had heard of your exploits with the Skraelings at Straumsfjord and I did not believe them. But now I see you are courageous as any man. I respect that."

He steps around and cuts the ropes on my wrists, and when my creaking arm falls free, I nearly jump upward in agony. He manipulates it gently into a piece of wool which he wraps around my neck like a sling.

"We will sleep now, and I promise I will not force you, because where would be the fun in that? But when your arm has healed and you return to your full power…well, things might be different then." He gestures to Kitta. "I'm going to sell this bleater to my men, but you are a different class of woman altogether."

I glare at him. "I am married."

"I doubt it you are now. I hate to tell you, but my men are well-trained and your husband likely didn't survive their attack. But no more talking. I need to rest. Both of you women, shut your mouths."

As he wraps himself in the only blanket by the fire, I glance toward Kitta. She has finally slumped to the ground, her half-burned body curled up like a bug. She moans frequently, as if her face were still on fire.

Compassion for the abused woman washes over me again. I find myself praying she will live to have a happy life, even if I cannot. At least I will die having known the love of my father, my daughter, and, in the end, my husband.

FORTY-ONE

BEFORE I EVEN START to dream, daylight streams onto my face and the Icelander nudges me awake with his boot. It should comfort me that he is taking a gentler approach this morning, but I know what he plans for me, so I groan loudly as if my arm is worse.

Actually, today my arm feels bruised and swollen, but not broken. I hide any traces of hope on my face, but I know that given the right moment, I might be able to overtake our captor.

He does not wake Kitta as I thought he would. Instead, he leans over and unties my feet. "Get up," he commands.

Alertness floods my senses. He wants me to walk somewhere, alone with him.

I consider methods of attack as I feign clumsiness, struggling to my feet. He's hidden my knife, so there's no chance of using that. After crying in pain throughout the night, Kitta has finally fallen into an exhausted sleep, so I cannot count on her help.

My legs are strong enough, and I might be able to kick out his knee if he stood behind me. It seems a weak option, especially since he would still have both hands free to grab a weapon. Meanwhile, I have only one hand I can count on right now.

When I finally stand, he moves behind me, shoving me with his hand. "Walk."

I obey but take my time. "Where are we going?"

"I thought we could check on your horse—you did bring one, didn't you?"

"He's probably gone by now."

"Let's go check," he says.

We walk in silence into the open field. I lead him toward the rocks, hoping the stallion has returned to the farm to alert Ref—if Ref is still alive.

"I am Hinrik," he says abruptly.

I don't respond. It is not good that he wants to tell me his name.

I trip in a patch of taller grass and fall to my knees. In a moment, he is behind me, trying to shove me to the ground.

"Last night I decided I would not wait for this." His breath is on my hair as he pushes my body flat. He sits on my back, but not with his full weight.

"Last night I decided not to wait for this, either." I twist in the space beneath him, flipping myself over. Using my good hand, I drive a sharp stick I picked up into his gut.

His eyes widen, but he quickly yanks the stick out. It must have barely penetrated his leather vest. He pushes my arms down. "You are everything I'd hoped for."

I have to stay alive for Kitta. Maybe if I become docile he won't be interested in me. But I don't have it in me to give in. I will die fighting.

I close my eyes so I don't have to see his face. Perhaps my instincts will show me a way out.

Suddenly, Hinrik's body is lifted from me. Maybe his men have found us, which would be even worse.

I cringe into the sunlight, making out a man on horseback who is holding Hinrik aloft by his vest. Several other horsemen sit around, but I can't see their faces clearly in the blinding morning light.

One of the horsemen jumps off and strides toward me. I roll over into a ball. This time I have no stick and no way of escape.

There is a soft touch on my hair, then a familiar voice wraps me like a healing balm. "Freydis. It's me."

My husband is alive, and for the first time, he has saved me.

༄

Thorfinn sits astride the lead horse. He drops Hinrik and jumps to the ground beside him, giving the Icelander a hard kick before he walks toward me.

"I am sorry for what you had to endure, Freydis. Mother and I escaped through our tunnel. Kitta couldn't get out before the entrance collapsed, so she ran out the door instead—straight into the arms of this hellion. Is she safe?"

I nod, motioning toward the trees with my head. I am too exhausted to explain the failure of my rescue attempt.

Understanding flashes across Thorfinn's face and he walks toward the trees. Ref pulls the groveling Icelander up with one hand so his men can tie him up. Atli joins him, and they toss Hinrik across a horse. He flails about in the same position he put Kitta in last night.

I wonder if the Holy Book mentions how heartening it can be to see evildoers receive punishment for their deeds. Or if it mentions how satisfying it can feel to bring such punishment about.

Ref comes and squats beside me. He holds my hand, and my old, inexplicable resentment toward his attentiveness rears its head. Why can't I accept his help and be thankful for it? Why can't I revel in his attentions instead of charging off on my own, looking for acceptance elsewhere?

"You are tired," he says, gripping my hand tighter.

"Yes."

"Amoda is safe. Dagmar practically mauled the man I sent to find her. He said the old woman had the strength of a berserker and the wildness to match."

I can't help but smile at the image of the white-haired woman, jumping out from among the sheep to protect my child.

I look at Hinrik, shuddering to think what he might have done with no fear of me or of my brother. "What will happen to him?"

"Thorfinn will take him to the Althing because of his intent to murder and for the damage to his longhouse."

"Does Gudrid know of this attack?"

"We sent a rider over this morning. She will likely come to see the devastation today."

"And help clean it up, knowing her."

"She is a good woman," he reflects. He kisses my hand. "But not my kind of woman."

I want to ask if his kind of woman is soft, but something holds me back.

The men bring Kitta from the woods, and in the light of day, I can see the permanent damage the fire has done to her beautiful face. What a sad course for her life—she left home in hopes of a productive future, only to find herself used and discarded, time and again.

Catching sight of me, she runs and drops to the ground next to me. She hugs me and kisses my cheek, giving a gasp of pain as her raw, blistering skin touches mine.

"Thank you for coming for me," she says.

I shake my head. "Don't thank me. I failed."

Her blue eyes are luminous, filled with clear admiration. "No. From the moment you saddled that horse to the moment you fell from the tree, you showed that you valued my life even more than your own. This is not the first time you have protected me. I will stay by your side forever."

Ref rubs at his nose and stands, uncomfortable. How things have twisted. Now his one-time lover declares her loyalty to his wife!

"Dagmar and Huld are old and you will need someone to look after your children," she continues. She carefully touches the burned skin on her face. "Look at me. I do not have a future as a wife."

"Do not say that. God has spared you for some purpose." I am talking to her as much as to myself.

"I will not leave you unless you make me," she says.

I look at Ref, who stands with his hands on his hips watching Hinrik squirm. Are we together as husband and wife, or does he plan to leave me as soon as possible? Perhaps our communion in the bath-house meant nothing to him.

He turns and meets my gaze. My body seems to respond of its own will and I take his outstretched hand to stand. I turn to Kitta. "I will consider your wish. I will pray about it."

Ref's eyebrows raise. "Pray about it?"

"I have much to tell you, Ref—if you will stay to hear it."

He kisses my forehead. "Where else would I go? I have sailed all the way to Iceland, haven't I?"

He does not add that he sailed here for me, but he doesn't have to. I read it in the light in his eyes, the hope in his voice. But there is some part of me that still pulls back from such adoration, and I am not sure I can ever accept it.

FORTY-TWO

WEEKS PASS AND THE warmth of summer folds into the chills of winter without a backward glance. Thorfinn's men have returned from their trading, just in time to help rebuild the longhouse.

Gudrid and I sit, taking a rare moment from packing turf onto the boards of the new house. I chew a strip of dried cod while she eats white cheese on flatbread. Our younger children play together in my house with Kitta, who seems determined to make good on her promise of lifelong allegiance to me. I think she would even agree to lifelong servitude, should I ask for it.

Abruptly, Gudrid speaks. "Runa asked me to live on the farm—but only if you stay with us. She was impressed with what a warrior you are, Freydis, and she wants you to protect the farm."

I laugh. "Do you really want to live so close to your mother-in-law?"

She chews her food, reflecting. "It is something I have asked God about many times. But I cannot see how we can share the same man. She wants Finn to keep the farm running, but I need him to keep our family together. I believe that is more important."

I nod. "You are right. She can find another man to run her farm."

"Or a woman?" She winks at me, then continues. "You are blessed. Your man sees only you and your needs." Her green gaze sharpens. "I know you do not care for being doted on—you run from it—but it is a blessing."

"How amusing that God has given us husbands who do the opposite of what we want. I want to be free from cloying love, while you would welcome it."

She fingers the embroidery on her yellow overdress. "Are you going to let Ref live with you again?"

For the past few weeks, Ref has slept in a longhouse with Atli and his men. Many times he has hinted that he would like to share my bed again, but I am not ready yet. Although I have forgiven Kitta and I've determined to protect her like one of my own brood, it is not so simple to forgive Ref, despite his begging.

"I am unsure." I watch my husband as he helps one of Thorfinn's men set a beautifully carved door into the doorframe. I know Ref has stayed up late working on this dark wood door, hoping to make this new longhouse as impressive as the original.

Gudrid follows my gaze. "Why do you hesitate?"

"I have too many concerns. What if he was the one who betrayed me to Leif? And he sought comfort in another woman's arms. What would happen if your Thorfinn did that?"

I know I am goading her, but her prying makes me irritable.

She never addresses my impertinence, but lets it slide off her, smooth as cream sliding off the milk.

"I cannot say what I would do, but I can say this—it is easy to fall into temptation, and Ref does not have the restraining hand of

God in his life. You have been forgiven of everything, Freydis, even murder. Could you not forgive your husband who hasn't abandoned you, who has sailed across the ocean to see you again, and who loves Amoda as much as you do? He has no interest in Kitta—she is a child. She will find someone else."

"And I will not?" If I were a wolf, my hair would be bristling on end now.

She laughs. "You are looking for a fight, I see. You know I won't fight you."

I slump into my chair, huffing. "I could find another man. I believe Thorgrim wanted me."

"That brute you sailed with? Really, Freydis. Don't lie to yourself. You do not need a man like that."

I tear off a piece of cod with my teeth, and Gudrid laughs again. "And now I expect you will sulk the rest of the day."

I don't know why she thinks she can speak to me this way. I stand, ready to stalk off, but Thorfinn walks over. His tunic is dirty, as is his face, but his eyes are soft as they rest on Gudrid.

"Mother wants to know if we should build a separate room in the longhouse for you and the boys."

"You would be with me? On our own bed?" Gudrid's voice is wary.

He shrugs. "I do not know. Perhaps it would take time."

Gudrid's voice gets dangerously low. "Time? We have been married for years. We have had children together. We do not need time. *I* need time with you, Thorfinn Karlsefni. And you will make time for me."

An uncomfortable silence falls. Gudrid won't run away from this discussion, as I would. She will stay until she gets her way, likely convincing Thorfinn that it was his idea in the first place.

"I will check on the children," I say. It is good for these two to talk and heal their marriage.

Perhaps I should do the same.

As I walk into my longhouse, Amoda tiptoes up to me. She loves being barefoot and has excellent balance. She stretches her arms toward me, dimpling into a smile.

Bjorn sits on the rug, babbling along to Kitta. The plump boy is built like a little bear, whereas my daughter is long and lean, like me.

When Kitta turns to me, I start afresh at the sight of her burned face. She sees my reaction and lowers her eyes before speaking.

"Amoda ate her mid-day meal, m'lady, and she will be ready for a nap soon. Shall I stay with the children?"

Before I can answer, there is a knock on the door. I open it to find Ref outside, his eyes hopeful as he looks from me to Amoda. My daughter squirms and squeals for her father, but I hold her tightly as Ref speaks.

"Perhaps I could lie down here for a short time? The men are eating in our house and I am weary."

He does not sound overly exhausted. He merely wants to come into my longhouse.

Yet something prods me to agree. I turn to Kitta.

"Please take Bjorn to his mother and find a place he can nap—perhaps in one of the smaller huts. I will stay here with Amoda."

Kitta hides it well, but her eyes flick beyond me to Ref. What did he give her that she so desperately needed? She could have had any of my crew or Leif's men, but she chose my husband.

I jerk my head away from her, repulsed again by their closeness.

Ref sees the unintentional curl of my lip and turns to go.

"Stay," I command. I turn to Kitta, who still sits on the rug. "Go."

Gathering Bjorn up in her arms, she brushes past me without a word. Is she upset with me? Before, I would not have cared if she was. But sympathy for Kitta's plight has dulled my detachment.

Ref hesitates, then boldly steps forward. "May I come in?"

I give a short nod. "Come."

Amoda screeches and lunges again for her father, back arched and arms outstretched. She is ready to tumble into his strong arms, and I allow her to go to him.

He kisses her repeatedly and she wraps an arm around his neck, stroking his beard as if it were her favorite toy. I cannot deny that Ref loves his daughter and knows how to be a good father to her.

Positioning himself next to her on the rug, he gives her toys and waits for me to speak.

I am not sure where to begin, so I ask God to help me. Whether we reconcile or whether our futures diverge, we must settle how things stand between us.

FORTY-THREE

I SINK ONTO THE bed. "Much has happened."

He keeps his head lowered, ready for my accusations. "Yes."

"I have thought much on our time in Vinland. You helped me with the Icelanders, and I want to thank you for standing by me."

He looks up, surprised. "Of course I would not let those men harm you."

"There is more to the story," I say. "In fact, I might have lied to you. I hate liars and I do not want lies between us. Yet I felt I had to do it to gain your support for the battle."

"Kitta explained when we were in Greenland," he says.

My back stiffens. "She explained *what*?"

"She said you loved Suka. She told me Valdis murdered him, so you took vengeance on the volva and the Icelanders."

"She lied!" I roar.

His gaze hardens. "It hurt me, hearing that you had been with the Skraeling."

"So you retaliated by rushing into Kitta's arms!" My voice grates, even on my own ears. "Well, she lied to you. I was never with Suka.

Yes, the volva killed Tyr's wife and they killed Suka. What Leif doesn't know—what no one knew—is that Valdis would have sailed to Greenland and killed my family there, as well. She was going to take *our child* when it was born, Ref, probably for another cannibal sacrifice. I could not have let that happen."

His anger finally surfaces. "She was a cannibal? Why didn't you tell me? I do not regret slaying that murderous crew—I am sure they wanted us dead. But tell me, how did you lie to me?"

"I misled you. The brothers did not harm me, but I know they would have. They would have followed her orders without question."

He leans against the bed, stroking my leg beneath my linen skirts. The feel of his rough palm on my skin is so familiar, so comforting, I am distracted when he finally speaks again.

"I suppose you told Leif none of this? He would not have been so quick to curse you for your actions if he'd known you were protecting Brattahlid, not to mention his own hide. Perhaps he would have let you buy the farm."

"That dream is dead." I tuck my legs beneath me so I can think. "He chose to believe the worst about me, to torture some made-up story out of someone—"

"I did it," he says simply.

My arms go numb. "You?"

"I told Leif what happened, but I was not thinking clearly. Kitta had just told me of your relationship with Suka, and I was furious that you led such a slaughter only to avenge your lover's death."

I pound the bed with both fists. "I...she will pay!"

He swings up to the bed beside me, his voice low. "What I cannot understand is why you didn't kill Kitta when you found her with me, or in the time since. It is good of you to let her live."

"And it is unlike me to spare her." I fill in the words he is thinking.

"Yes. But why? And why did you race to save her from the Icelanders here?"

I look up, taking in the blue sky through the smoke hole. "I have changed."

"I know this," he says, tracing the freckles on my cheeks.

"I have believed in the Christian God."

His hand drops as if he's been scalded by fire. "You tease me?"

Amoda clambers up on the bed beside me, ready for a nap. I draw her close. "I don't tease. Gudrid told me about the One who has the power to forgive every sin, even murder."

Ref runs a hand through his already-messy hair. "And this is something you need?"

He looks at me as if he can't believe what he's hearing.

Yes, I have finally admitted I need something. I've lied to myself all my life, so confident I could face every foe alone and build my own future.

But I needed forgiveness.

I needed acceptance.

I needed love.

Amoda pulls away from me and crawls up the bed, then rolls onto her side to sleep.

Ref laughs. "She knows what she wants, like her mother."

"And yet she is polite, like her father. She did not scream to get my attention, as I probably would have."

Ref stands and kisses my head. "Do not assume you were such a wayward child…although it's entirely possible you were a beautiful terror."

I laugh along with him. He yawns and I grow serious.

"You were not lying. You are tired."

"Of course," he says. "We have been working since the sun was up."

"Lie down with us, then. We will take a family nap. The bed is large enough."

He gives me a long look. "You are sure?"

I smile. "Take off your filthy tunic and trousers and wash with a wet cloth. Then you can surely share my bed…for a nap."

Nearly an hour later, a banging on the door wakes us. Ref opens it and I hear him greet Gudrid.

I walk over to meet her. Her hair is ruffled and her cheeks reddened, as if she has run to my house.

"Horsemen have arrived," she says.

"Icelanders?" I ask quickly.

"No. You will not believe me if I tell you."

I grab her forearm. "Tell me."

She gives me a cautious smile. "Greenlanders."

I look from her to Ref, disbelieving what I have heard. "Greenlanders? But who?"

Her smile becomes wider. "Only the most famous Greenlander of all. Your brother, Leif."

FORTY-FOUR

I HEAR MY BROTHER'S booming voice before I reach the new longhouse. He is dressed in a showy manner, wearing new boots and a cross on a silver chain around his neck. His long blond hair flows free, carefully cleaned and combed.

"Sister!" He turns from Thorfinn and strides toward me.

Amoda nearly jumps from my arms to see him. Instead, I grip her tighter and step back. Ref stands by my side and snakes his arm protectively around my waist. For once I do not mind.

Atli, too, comes from the longhouse and stands near me. He is showing his loyalty again, and I am reminded that despite his youth, he can fight as well as Leif himself. Atli wears an axe on his belt, standing aggressively with his feet planted wide.

Everyone fears Leif has come here to kill me. He could eliminate the blot I have brought to his name.

From the corner of my eye, I spot Thorgrim on one of the horses. He must have traveled with Leif. He gives me a wink, which might be a good sign. Or it might mean nothing.

Leif ignores Ref's glare and touches Amoda's cheeks. She

squeals in delight.

"Don't touch my daughter," I say. "Get this over with."

Leif gives me a wounded look. "Why do you think I have come?"

I hedge. "I couldn't say. No one ever knows what Leif Eiriksson will do next."

He squares his wide shoulders, and I hate how short I feel in his presence. "Freydis, Thorgrim sailed to me and reported what those house-burning Icelanders did to Thorfinn's farm. He told me they kidnapped one of your women?"

Why would Leif care about these things? He was the one who banished me to Iceland.

"I can take care of myself," I say.

Ref's arm tightens.

"And so will my husband," I add.

Leif looms closer. "Thorgrim thinks there is more to your slaughter in Vinland than what you told me. I came to hear the whole truth. I also came to speak on your behalf at the Icelandic Althing."

If I must go to the Althing, I can speak for myself, since I am a free woman. But the judges will not look favorably on me if they hear the full truth of what happened in Vinland.

"You do not own land here," I point out. "They will not want to hear you."

"No. You forget that Father loaned his farmland here, but he never sold it. It is rightfully mine."

Fury creeps up my face until my ears have turned as red as my cheeks. "Then it is also mine!"

He pauses to consider. "I suppose so. Actually, you're welcome to it. Rocky bit of land anyway, hard to farm."

"How thoughtful of you," I grind out.

Thorfinn steps closer. Gudrid has moved to his side, bouncing Bjorn on her hip. Predictably, Leif's eyes drift away from me to watch her.

I shove into his elbow to snap him out of his trance.

Thorfinn speaks up, unruffled by Leif's leering. He probably takes it as a matter of course now. "Let us have our evening meal together. Your men are welcome to help themselves to our drink and rest, but we need to finish sodding this roof today."

"We thank you," Leif says, offering an exaggerated bow. I give a little snort at his feigned respect.

Thorgrim trots closer, pulling his horse up near me. "There is to be an Althing in nine days. I have heard it from Leiknir in the village."

"You were in the village?" I ask.

"I was halfway across Iceland when I heard of the fire and raid on this farm. I rode to your village to see if it was true. When I found it was, they mentioned the Althing and I did not hesitate. I sailed immediately for Leif."

Ref gives Thorgrim a thoughtful look.

I have to ask. "You went to all this trouble for me?"

A dark lock of hair falls over Thorgrim's eye. "For you and your child. I did not realize—" He looks at Ref, stricken.

Ref nods as if he understands perfectly. So perfectly, he looks like he wants to chop Thorgrim's head off.

"Thank you." I force a tone of dismissal I do not feel.

Thorgrim takes a quick look at Ref and spurs his horse to the barn.

Leif pats my back. "We will see you at the evening meal then, Freydis. Don't fret. Your older brother is here."

Gudrid catches my eye, a twinkle in hers. We both nearly burst into laughter as Leif struts off to give his men instructions. As Thorfinn and Ref begin to discuss the best way to set the sod, Gudrid and I fall into step together.

"That is something I never saw coming," I say. "My older brother sailing in to speak on my behalf."

"I doubt you will need his help," Gudrid says. "Thorfinn and his mother will be believed over the troll who burned the farm and dragged Kitta off. That raider may think so highly of his family, but they mean nothing around here."

"But if anyone mentions the slaughter in Vinland, things could go very badly." I lay my hand on Amoda's curls, knowing my daughter will be motherless if the Althing rules against me.

Oblivious to my heartache, Amoda gives several regular, light kicks, letting me know she wants to walk on the grass. I reluctantly pull her from the sling, feeling an unreasonable, motherly urge to hold her forever. As I place her on the ground, Gudrid releases Bjorn from her grasp and the children begin to romp together.

Gudrid places a hand on mine, steadying me with her gaze. "God will work in the Althing meeting, I know. All the men will speak for you, even regarding the murders in Vinland, if you can convince Leif they were justified."

"Why don't you convince him for me?" I laugh, but I would not argue if Gudrid acted on my suggestion.

She shakes her head. "You need to do this. Before, you were too proud and stubborn to tell him the whole story. Now you must tell him everything. I will pray his heart will be open—and I believe it is."

"If only his heart were as open as yours, Gudrid. Then he wouldn't have banished me in the first place."

※

We take our evening meal on three long tables, the fresh sod roof stretching over us. Runa will move into this longhouse now. I wonder if Gudrid agreed to sleep in the same house as her mother-in-law, but I doubt it.

Runa looks over at Amoda and her eyes soften. She almost seems to have grown fond of having us around. After the fire destroyed her house, we have spoken daily—generally about nothing important, but sometimes she asks me questions about how we farmed at Brattahlid and how I learned to fight and sail. She almost seems to wish she could learn those things herself. I sense a wanderer's spirit in her that was never freed.

Perhaps I could have turned out the same as Runa, had my father not encouraged me to be bold. Gudrid has told me many times she wishes he would have treated me more like a lady and less like a son, but the faithful training of Eirik the Red has kept me alive, both in battle and on the seas. And I have kept others alive because of it.

Leif jabs me lightly with his finger. "You're lost in thought. Perhaps you are wondering why I came."

Of course he assumes I was thinking of him. Sometimes I think my brother is the center of his own world, despite his Christianity.

He pushes a bite of *dulse* into his mouth, the red sea lettuce coloring his teeth as he chews. Once he swallows it in one huge gulp, he speaks again. "I will tell you why. Mother came to me in a dream. Not just any dream, either. It was a dream that would not go away. Every night, there she was in some form or another, saying something about Freydis."

He arches a light eyebrow, as if daring me to contradict his tale.

I take him up on it.

"You say *Mother*. Are you speaking of Thjodhild, *your* dead mother? My mother was not married to your father, as I am sure you might recall."

He nods brusquely, impatient to continue his story. "Of course. She was your mother too, even though you never cared for her. Don't forget she saved you when you were just a babe, when the volva wanted to leave you out to the elements."

In those early days of Greenland, the volva ruled the land by fear, sometimes even demanding the lives of the jarls' babies. Valdis had planned to bring those days back.

One thing I will never understand—why Thjodhild saved me at all. And now Leif tells me the icy woman has haunted him in dreams, leading him back to me? It is hard to believe.

Gudrid, who has been sitting in silence next to me, leans in toward my ear. "God works miracles, and He sometimes works through dreams. Do not forget, Thjodhild was a Christian, so she is still alive in another place."

Leif waits for Gudrid to finish whispering, then he speaks again. "Thanks to those dreams, I realized I had done wrong by you. I never offered you a chance to explain the actions you took in Vinland, as I would have offered any of my men."

I sneer. "So you suddenly realized you should treat me like an equal? You should have done that when I sailed back, ship laden with goods from Vinland. You should have let me buy the farm and enrich your empty money chests. You and Thorstein should not have taunted me for being a girl when I was small."

Where did that come from? I haven't thought of Leif's taunting and Thorstein's pranks since I was young. Gudrid gives me a sad look, as if she was unaware of my brothers' harshness to me.

Leif, too, is taken aback for a moment, then he recovers his usual bluster. "Just tell me what happened in Vinland."

I should have known he would never fully apologize.

But I will tell him, if only to strengthen my position at the Althing. I must have some protection in place in case the Althing judges learn the truth.

FORTY-FIVE

FOR SEVEN DAYS, I fast from food, taking drink only.

For seven days, Gudrid prays for me.

For seven days, my husband tries to comfort me by spending time with Amoda. It has rained steadily during this time, and my daughter does not like being trapped inside. But when Ref is around, she cheers up, playing contentedly with her wooden hammer and blocks.

Yet still I ask him to sleep in the men's longhouse. It is better for him if he holds me loosely in case things take a bad turn at the Althing.

On the seventh day, we assemble our traveling party, since it will take nearly a day to travel to the site. The old women and Gudrid will stay with the children. Kitta will accompany us, since she must speak against Hinrik, who will be brought to the Althing by the jailers in the village.

Leif's warriors have joined with Thorfinn's to represent the unified strength of their farms. They will make an impressive showing.

Thorfinn slaps Leif on the shoulder as they pack the horses. "I am not sure how your laws are in Greenland, but I hope the Icelandic chieftains agree to let you act as one of them—a *goði*—listening to our laws and amending them. You will also speak before the judges on our behalf about why we were forced to kill Hinrik's raiders. I will speak, as well. Although I have resisted becoming chieftain because of my frequent travels, my word will be respected in the assembly."

Leif nods seriously, and for a moment I am actually fond of my brother. He listened to my account of what happened in Vinland and said little, but his narrowed eyes and clenched jaw spoke for him. He likely would have killed Valdis himself, had he been in my position.

I am praying that only Hinrik's raid will be discussed, and not the motives behind it. As a free man, Hinrik will be allowed to speak, and he will doubtless rant about his brothers' murders in Vinland.

But no one can prove that any of the Icelanders died there.

Ref saddles our horse and boosts me onto it before falling into step next to me. Horses are limited here, and he insists I ride for most of our journey.

This sort of demand would have bothered me before. I would have ranted about how I was able to walk every bit as far as Ref and I would have demanded someone else use our horse.

Now I see my senseless excuses for what they were—a cloak for my competitiveness. An inability to let myself feel weak, even for a moment.

The truth is more difficult. I am weak sometimes. I fell from a tree into my captor's hands, instead of slitting his throat. I was helpless to stop my husband from sharing his bed with Kitta. I did not protect Suka from Valdis' grasp.

And though I might not fear battling anyone, the fear of being forced to leave my daughter controls my heart right now.

Ref seems to understand my need for silence, and I am thankful he is not a chattering man, like Leif. It does not take long for me to grow weary of my brother's voice as he boasts to the other warriors who travel with us. I am not the only one. Thorfinn avoids Leif and Kitta skulks to the rear of the traveling party when Leif is talking.

We travel along the river, arriving at the *Thingvellir* fields by nightfall. Thorfinn locates our fellow villagers and they lead us to a grouping of small stone foundations we will use as bases for our tents.

Once we have built a roaring fire and bought some of the heartening ale from the on-site brewhouse vendors, Kitta asks me where she will sleep for the night. I am the only other woman, and much as I hope to protect her, I know she cannot stay with Ref and me. Most of the men cannot be trusted to keep their hands off her, including my brother. And though I don't believe Thorfinn would stray from Gudrid, I don't want to put him in that position.

Finally, Atli speaks up, offering to share a tent with her. They are already friends, he says, and he seeks nothing more than her safety. When I see the relief in her eyes, I quickly agree to the arrangement.

Once our tents are built, Ref and I crawl into ours, rolling out our sleep sacks. In the morning, Ref will join the others to catch fish for our mid-day meal, since the nearby lake is teeming with them.

Much as I dread the morrow, I feel strangely elated to be alone with my husband. Our sleeping quarters are so close, we are practically pushing into one another each time we move. But the darkness seems to blanket my fear, loosening my tongue. Or perhaps it is the good ale that probably went straight to my head after days of fasting.

"If they hear about Vinland, they will never forgive me," I say. "Will you marry Kitta if I am condemned to death?"

Ref does not hesitate. "No. I do not love her."

"But what if I asked you to marry her? She would be loyal to Amoda, in deference to my memory."

Ref chuckles. "I think I would have to fight off her admirer. Our young Atli is very committed to her well-being, and perhaps wishes he could be permanently committed to her by marriage, as well."

"You think so? Was I wrong to let them sleep in the same tent?"

Ref drops his hand on my forehead, stroking my hair. "No. Atli will be honorable. He knows of her past and would never force her." His tone deepens. "Now it is my turn to question you. What if you are not condemned, how will you live then? Would you allow me to be a husband to you again?"

I have wondered that myself, but I cannot allow myself to hope for freedom on the other side of the Althing meeting. I must plan for the worst, so I cannot anticipate the best.

I long to be a wife to Ref and a mother to Amoda. Nothing else matters anymore.

If I say this, if I admit my need to Ref, some twisted part of me knows that it will not happen. Some are born to love, and some to fight. How can I ever succeed at both?

I roll over, out from under his hand.

He does not move for a moment, then he searches for my forehead in the dark and once again places his hand on it. His words plunge into my heart, deeper than any arrow.

"Freydis, why won't you let me love you?"

Wild emotions well up, threatening to destroy who I have always been. A forest child, lacking position and respect, lacking the abundant love of a mother or siblings, lacking in looks. A godless rebel, ready to fight my way out of any situation. A heartless woman who can cleave another woman's head without having a second thought about it.

A warrior, honed and sharp.

But now I have a God. I have a daughter I cannot be without. And I have a husband who yearns to fill me with the love I have lacked.

My words come out hoarsely, as if they have been torn from my throat. "I will let you love me."

My husband slides from his sleep sack, enfolding me in his arms. I lie there for the longest time, weeping tears I never knew I had.

FORTY-SIX

REF BRINGS ME COOKED fish before the crowds gather at the Law Rock. I am quite sure we are smiling at each other like two who have been newly married. Perhaps we have finally been *truly* married in a way we never were before.

As we approach the meeting area, it is easy to recognize the Lawspeaker because he is alone. He stands on a raised, flat rock, and is surrounded by a rock wall so his voice will carry as he recites the laws. He wears a red tunic so he will be easily seen.

Leif is dressed in his favorite blue tunic, a heavy gold chain and ruby encrusted cross around his neck. The king of Norway gave him this showy adornment to show his support for Leif's missionary efforts in Greenland.

Leif strides over to join the group of *goðar* who stand below the Lawspeaker. Below these chieftains, the judges sit in circles. They will hear our individual disputes.

I can see the men are impressed with my brother, probably because of his favor with the Norwegian king. There is much nodding and smiling, along with friendly thumps on the back, then Leif returns to our group.

"They said it was only last year that they began to open the Althing with a Christian prayer, instead of their pagan runes and chants. Many of the lawgivers have already converted, and they wish to maintain favor in their trading with the Norwegians and Danes. What is more, they have asked me to offer the prayer today!"

We congratulate Leif, though I wonder just what kind of prayer my brother will offer. I hope he doesn't unwittingly offend the Icelanders and ruin our chances of winning our disputes.

~

After Leif's prayer, which pleases everyone, the sun seems to move quickly through the sky. Vendors make their way through the crowds, offering dried meats, pastries, and ale, but I partake of nothing. My stomach is heaving and I know that anything I eat will come back up.

Finally, the chieftains give the command and we separate into judgment circles where we will speak our grievances.

When our turn comes, Hinrik speaks first. He has only a few men left to speak for him, because most of his men were killed the night of their raid.

He spits out his tale, saying Eirik the Red's daughter killed his brother to steal his ship. He insinuates that I am bloodthirsty and perhaps inhuman. He finishes by saying that Kitta and I lured him into the woods to perform evil deeds and to put curses upon him.

As he tells this lie, Ref squeezes my hand so hard it hurts, holding back from attacking the man who is defaming my name.

All eyes are on Kitta's fire-scarred face as she stands to offer her testimony. She looks guileless in her plain white shift and a green overdress, complemented only by simple metal brooches. She tells the story exactly as it happened, and I believe a judge would have to be heartless not to believe her plaintive tale.

I look around the circle. There is a red-bearded man who reminds me of my father, sitting with a wife who looks sympathetic to Kitta. There are younger men who must be only eighteen, the age required to become judge. There are shepherds and sailors, farmers and weavers, and free men of all types.

When I am called to speak, I focus on our men, and it is encouraging. Atli beams at me. Thorfinn, Leif, and Ref give the impression of wealth. Thorgrim and my sailors are here to back my story, no matter what I choose to say.

I speak loudly so everyone can know I am not ashamed. "Hinrik the Spineless has told you one story, and the girl Kitta has told you another. I will now tell you the truth before God."

Murmurs rumble through the crowd. It is risky, naming the Christian God, for some still put their faith in the pagan gods and might hate me for it. But I am willing to take the chance, calling on the highest power there is. I know that Christian monks have performed miracles in Iceland that have made the volva look weak.

I continue. "What Kitta has said is right and all our men will say the same. Hinrik invaded Thorfinn Karlsefni's vast and admirable farm without warning. He burned the longhouse, intending to trap and kill everyone in it, including Karlsefni." I deliberately use Thorfinn's last name, to show him a respect I have not volunteered before. "Thankfully, my husband and his men rallied and stopped the raiders before they were able to burn more houses or people. It was the hand of God that spared Kitta and allowed Karlsefni and his mother, Runa, to escape."

One of the men in the crowd stands. He has a thick neck and bald head. "And what of Hinrik's claim he owed you vengeance for stealing his brother's ship? Is it true the ship was sold in Iceland by one of your crew?"

I have sworn by God to tell the truth, so I will. "Yes. I ordered him to sell it."

The man chuckles and turns to the judges. "We can believe her story, friends, because I am the jarl who bought that ship."

I whisper a thanks to God and speak on. "I did not steal the ship. It was…promised to me."

A man near Hinrik stands. He is clad in a tattered fur vest with no tunic, and his hands are fixed squarely on his hips as he glares at me. "And you want us to believe that Helgi, Finnbogi, and our Icelandic friends stayed behind in Vinland?"

I have thought about describing my retaliatory actions, telling the Icelanders the entire story of Valdis' evil deeds. Perhaps it would assuage my guilt, but it would only place Gudrid and her family in a tenuous position with the Icelanders she has settled with. I cannot put them in danger. So I have prayed that God will allow me to answer the questions without lying.

This seems to be my opportunity.

"Believe what you want about those who sailed alongside us." I force myself to meet the eyes of every judge. Perhaps they will catch the flash of righteous anger in my eyes, sense my determination to maintain silence about Vinland.

Ref stands before the surly man can probe further. "We had to return, as my wife was with child and wanted to go home to Greenland."

Leif takes his turn. "My sister and her crew sailed into Brattahlid last spring, and she was nothing but helpful to me during that time. She hunts better than my men and kept our farm supplied with meat. Her crew were a boon to my people, chopping wood and fishing. This troll, Hinrik, must be punished for his misguided and deadly attack on Thorfinn Karlsefni's farm and on my esteemed sister."

I keep my expression calm, but inside, I want to shout with joy. My brother, who has never appreciated me openly before, has just given a speech on my strengths and called me *esteemed*. I remain standing, even as a light rain begins to fall.

Thorfinn Karlsefni speaks last. "Ask anyone—our longhouse was fitted with beautiful wood from Vinland and Straumsfjord. I have brought nothing but wealth to our region because I was not afraid to sail to the new lands Leif Eiriksson had found. I am one of the most respected traders in Norway and beyond. And this rogue—this merciless fool—decided to attack us." He points at Kitta's face. "Look what he has done to this woman! He would have burned me alive, as well as my mother! He must suffer consequences and make restoration."

Hinrik stands and calls down curses from the skies above and the seas below. His own man has to pull him back down to his place on the bench.

The red-bearded older man holds up a hand and stands. "I have heard enough. Hinrik took this idea into his head—that because this woman sold Helgi's ship, she must have killed him. A free man has every right to sell his ship to another, and I, for one, believe the daughter of Eirik the Red."

His wife stands. "I, too, believe the woman."

I hold my breath, praying. It might come to this—those who are for me stand, and those who are against me remain seated.

One after another, like a wave sweeping the water, people stand. The red-bearded man gives me a wink, and it is as if I can feel the warmth of my father's approval once again. It only takes a moment and nearly every judge has stood in my favor.

This is one of the most astonishing moments of my life. The moment when the forest child was allowed to speak and her words were respected. The moment when evildoers will be punished and I am not the only one who sees the need for it.

Ref and Leif flank me, two strong men who have chosen to stay by my side. The red-bearded man suggests Hinrik be banished from Iceland, and the judges agree. Even the Lawspeaker steps in when all has been decided, proclaiming Hinrik an outcast.

As I raise my face to the sunlight shafting through the rain clouds, a rainbow catches my eye. It is not a coincidence. It is the smile of God.

FORTY-SEVEN

OUR JOURNEY HOME IS filled with rejoicing, all our warriors jubilant that Hinrik will suffer for his rampant destruction.

Kitta makes her way to my side as our horses rest and eat. She looks as if she slept soundly, which is encouraging.

"Atli treated you well?" I ask.

"He did, m'lady." She looks down, waiting for me to say more.

I do have more to say. I have been filled with new resolve after the Althing.

"I believe you need to return home," I say. "Your family needs to know you live."

"But—"

I interrupt her. "You know you cannot stay with Ref and me, much as you love Amoda. You must forge your own path now, and you cannot let anyone do this for you."

"I will have no future," she says.

"That is a lie. You could have a future with one of the best warriors in Iceland." I motion to Atli, who is sparring swords with Thorfinn.

She blushes.

"If he asks you to marry him, you should say yes. Of course, no one can decide for you, but I believe you care for him?"

Her blush deepens, still lovely under her scarred skin. "I do."

I am sure Atli will ask her, because today he spoke with Ref about what would make a good betrothal gift. I hope my hint makes Kitta examine her feelings and prepare for this opportunity.

I continue. "I free you from any obligation or promise to me. I want you to live a full life, as I have."

She gives a reluctant nod, but her eyes are bright. "Thank you."

As she takes her horse to watch the men, I drop onto the grassy knoll and lean back on my hands. I have a feeling Kitta and Atli will be a strong couple, like Gudrid and Thorfinn. And I have begun to see that Ref and I might be one of those couples, as well.

Gudrid emerges from the longhouse on our return, Amoda in her arms. She examines my face, then shouts. "You have not been condemned!"

We hug each other, and she passes Amoda to me. Ref steps closer, and our daughter immediately leans into his arms.

I try to express my thanks. "Your husband's word was worth so much."

Gudrid smiles. "I knew it would be."

"As was my brother's," I continue, shooting Leif a thankful look. He arches an eyebrow and grins in return.

Runa also comes to greet us, approaching Thorfinn first. "Gudrid and I have spoken," she says.

Thorfinn hides his surprise well. "Indeed?"

"And we have decided that you must build your own farm, Finn. There is good land not far from here that would be perfect."

Thorfinn's gaze travels immediately to Gudrid.

His wife speaks. "Runa began to see how distracted you were, with your family living in the village. She does not think you can do your best work this way."

Runa nods. "What if you had been killed in the fire? Your children would have been fatherless. They need you with them."

I cover my smile with my hand, feigning a yawn. This is Gudrid's work. She may be a Christian now, but she can still manipulate minds like a volva.

Runa adds to my astonishment by wrapping an arm around my shoulder. "I would like a woman to oversee my farm. A woman who could rally my men. I am looking for a woman like you, daughter of Eirik the Red."

Ref's gaze sweeps the farm, and I know he would like me to consider this option. It would be peaceful here, now that Hinrik is banished. We could make a name for ourselves.

Leif dismounts, edging past Runa none too gently. "I have a counter-offer. I would like you to buy into Brattahlid, Freydis. Now that I see you were protecting it all along, I would not be ashamed to share it with you—perhaps even sell to you in time."

I feel like a child who has been given two equally enticing toys. It is impossible to know which to choose.

"I must talk with Ref," I say, taking hold of my husband's sleeve. Amoda clings to him as I lead us toward the field.

We will go to the forest where I can think. I know Leif will sail soon, and I must have an answer for him. But I will make no decisions without my husband.

※

I do not speak a word until we are standing under a canopy of yellowing leaves. "You have thoughts on this, Ref?"

He gives me a carefully blank stare. "I will go with what you choose. I know you have dreamed all your life to own Brattahlid. Now things are smooth between you and Leif, so this is your chance."

"Yes, but is it the right decision, do you think?"

He gazes into the trees, thinking of what to say to me.

I nudge him. "I do not want you to hesitate. What do you feel is right?"

He leans forward, touching my cheek, then letting his finger trail to my chin. Amoda giggles in his arms.

"I will not hate you for saying what you think," I add.

"My dream has always been the same," he says slowly. "For us to be a family. As long as we are one now, I do not care where we settle."

"But if you had your choice?" I persist.

He glances around. A waterfall roars in the distance. Amoda reaches for the tree limbs, and he carefully places her on a low, strong branch, gripping her tight.

"I would choose to stay here," he says, and his answer resonates in my own spirit.

My daughter sits snug in her father's arms, enjoying the light sway of the branch. I see no reason to move her. She is no forest child, left alone in the trees to care for herself. She is surrounded by love—the love of her father and mother, the love of her family. She is happy and content.

Just as I am.

"It was Karlsefni who gave the most extensive reports of anyone of all of these voyages, some of which have now been set down in writing."
-*The Saga of the Greenlanders*

GLOSSARY

Althing: General parliamentary assembly held outdoors in Viking times—one of the oldest parliamentary institutions in the world

Dulse: Red alga (like seaweed)

Goði: Chieftains who appointed judges for the Althing

Helheim: Hell

Hross: Horse

Jarl: Earl

Knarr: Wider, deeper ship than the longship, used for sea voyages and trading

Lawspeaker: Elected for three years, presided over the Althing, and recited the laws aloud

Modi: Mother

Norns: Mythical women who weave threads of destiny (similar to Fates)

Sami: Nomadic reindeer herders of Lapland

Skraelings: Word the Vikings used for indigenous peoples from Greenland and the New World

Skyr: Cultured dairy product similar in consistency to yogurt

Thingvellir: Assembly plains where the Althing was held

Volva: Viking pagan seeress or holy woman

FREYDIS' FAMILY TREE:

Father: Eirik the Red (dead)

Mother: Unknown mistress of Eirik

Stepmother: Thjodhild, Eirik's Christian wife (dead)

Half-brother: Thorvald, brunette son of Eirik/Thjodhild who was killed in the New World in a Skraeling attack (dead)—he was married to Stena

Half-brother: Thorstein, red-haired son of Eirik/Thjodhild who was married to Gudrid for a short time (dead)

Half-brother (Eirik's son): Leif, blond son of Eirik/Thjodhild who married Gunna of the Hebrides when she told him she was carrying his son, Gils; Leif was also the first to explore the New World and he established a camp at Vinland

Sister-in-law: Gudrid, twice-widowed wife of Thorir the Eastman (dead), Thorstein Eiriksson (dead), and finally of Thorfinn Karlsefni; Gudrid adopted Skraeling boys named Hellir and Hol, also had sons Snorri and Bjorn with Thorfinn

Sister-in-law: Stena, Sami reindeer herder from Lapland who married Thorvald

Husband: Ref (his real name was Thorvard, but I changed it to something shorter for this series)

Daughter: Amoda

Other Characters:

Valdis: Icelandic volva married to Finnbogi

Finnbogi: Icelander who loaned a ship to Freydis

Helgi: Icelandic brother of Finnbogi

Kitta: Icelander trained as a volva

Suka: Native Greenlander who stayed in the New World after the previous voyage (in *God's Daughter*)

Tyr: Warrior who stayed in the New World after the previous voyage (in *God's Daughter*)

Atli: Norwegian warrior teen Freydis is training

ABOUT THE AUTHOR:

HEATHER DAY GILBERT, a Grace Award winner and bestselling author, writes novels that capture life in all its messy, bittersweet, hope-filled glory. Born and raised in the West Virginia mountains, generational story-telling runs in her blood. Heather is a graduate of Bob Jones University and is married to her college sweetheart. Having recently returned to her roots, she and her husband are raising their three children in the same home in which Heather grew up.

Heather's Viking historical novel, *God's Daughter*, is an Amazon Norse Bestseller. *Forest Child* is Book 2 in the Vikings of the New World Saga. Heather is also the author of the bestselling *A Murder in the Mountains* mystery series. Her mystery, *Trial by Twelve*, was the 2015 Grace Award winner for Mystery/Romantic Suspense/Thriller/Historical Suspense. Heather also authored the *Indie Publishing Handbook: Four Key Elements for the Self-Publisher*.

Please sign up for Heather's newsletter for sneak peeks of her upcoming releases here: **http://eepurl.com/Q6w6X**

For more information on Heather and her books, please check out **heatherdaygilbert.com**. Heather loves to hear from her readers, so please email her at heatherdaygilbert (at) gmail (dot) com with any thoughts on *Forest Child*.

Finally, reviews are always greatly appreciated—it's the perfect way to show authors they have touched your life with their stories. You can review *Forest Child* on Amazon, Barnes and Noble, Goodreads, and other online vendors. Thank you!

Made in the USA
Charleston, SC
02 March 2017